Nikki peeked in on Emma. "She's fast asleep," she said when she rejoined Galen in the living room.

"Are you hungry? How about a scoop of ice cream before you leave?"

"I'd rather taste something sweeter."

"What would that be?" she managed to choke out in a hoarse voice.

"I'll show you."

He pulled her close and took her mouth in one smooth action that left her reeling. Then he stopped abruptly, but his hold didn't slacken. For several long minutes he simply stared at her, his face wreathed in shadows as he waited silently.

She hadn't realised until that moment how hard it must have been for him to walk away a year ago, because refusing the unspoken question shining out of his eyes required a strength she didn't possess. Perhaps he'd changed, as he'd said, and perhaps he hadn't. But weren't some things in life worth the risk?

Dear Reader

Welcome to my **HOPE CITY** series, where people find love as they pursue their dreams and aspirations.

The idea for this series grew out of the knowledge that we've all entertained hopes at one time or another. So I wanted to create a town where my characters not only give hope to others through their profession, but, for various reasons, also cling to it themselves.

The Baby Rescue is the second story, where the bond that grows between two people who care for a baby really proves how important trust and dependability are in any relationship. Look for some of Hope City Hospital's other doctors—Mark Cameron and Justin St James—in future stories, where the combination of medicine and romance gives the community its name.

Happy reading!

Jessica Matthews

THE
BABY RESCUE

BY
JESSICA MATTHEWS

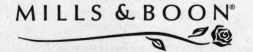

To Cathy and Barb, who kept me on track
when I thought I wasn't. Thanks.

Acknowledgements
My special thanks go to Alasdair Mearns,
for his information about bagpipes. Any errors are my own.

*All the characters in this book have no existence outside the imagination
of the author, and have no relation whatsoever to anyone bearing the
same name or names. They are not even distantly inspired by any
individual known or unknown to the author, and all the incidents are
pure invention.*

*First published in Great Britain 2004
Harlequin Mills & Boon Limited,
Eton House, 18-24 Paradise Road, Richmond, Surrey TW9 1SR*

© Jessica Matthews 2004

ISBN 0 263 83903 6

*Set in Times Roman 10½ on 12 pt.
03-0604-46507*

*Printed and bound in Spain
by Litografia Rosés, S.A., Barcelona*

CHAPTER ONE

"HAVING problems?"

Bent over the restroom doorknob with a hairpin in the key slot, Nicole Lawrence stiffened at the sound of the familiar baritone. After learning that Galen Stafford was a staff ER physician here at Hope City Hospital during yesterday's orientation tour, she'd been steeling herself for this moment when their awkward past would catch up to their equally awkward present.

Some might have considered it serendipitous for the two of them to land in the same hospital a year after they'd graduated from residency training, but Nikki did not. Of all the places she could have been sent to work, why did Galen have to be *here*?

Idly, she wondered if Emily Post or Miss Manners had ever covered the proper way to greet a man she'd once tried—and failed—to seduce.

She only wished their first face-to-face encounter since they'd parted company hadn't occurred at the exact moment her recalcitrant six-year-old patient had turned the restroom into his sanctuary. So much for proving her competence to a former fellow resident, even if he'd seen her in far worse situations than this.

Bluffing her way through was her only choice. It wouldn't be the first time she'd hidden something from him.

She straightened slowly as she turned to meet his gaze. Although she'd tried to mentally prepare herself for this moment, the magnetism she'd felt when she'd first met

5

him at St Luke's Medical Center in what seemed a lifetime ago instantly pulled at her. For a split second she weakened and drank in his appearance, letting herself remember only the good times they'd shared.

The love she'd felt for him, the love that she had been certain had withered over the past year, instantly stirred as if preparing to bloom. Determined to deny it, she forced herself to remember his rejection and her embarrassment after the night that could have become so special.

To give credit where it was due, he'd tried to soften the blow to her ego with an explanation, but by then she hadn't cared about his reasons, only the outcome. To save face, she'd hidden her hurt behind a practiced smile and had pretended that all had been well for their remaining weeks together.

It was time for a repeat performance.

"Hi, Galen. Long time no see," she said, hoping she sounded as warm and friendly as possible when she was irritated with herself for still suffering from an annoying case of unrequited love.

The lazy grin she remembered appeared on his handsome face as he eyed her from head to toe. "You haven't changed a bit."

"There's bound to be a few changes," she answered lightly. "Nothing stays the same."

"You're right," he agreed. "I've added a few wrinkles, a few gray hairs, and a few pounds." He patted an abdomen that seemed extremely trim in Nikki's opinion.

Those crinkles around his eyes didn't amount to much and she couldn't see any silver strands in his pecan-brown hair. As for the few pounds he'd added, they'd ended up in all the right places, filling out his tall form with muscles that would have done any athlete proud.

If she'd found him irresistible and had fancied herself

in love with him when they had been residents, she didn't have a chance at successfully fighting her attraction to him now.

"All for the better," she said politely, palming the hairpin as she tried to think of a way to send him on his way, both for her peace of mind and so she could return to the task at hand. Before she could put a coherent thought together, he pointed to the door.

"What's going on? Is the door stuck?"

"You could say that," she said slowly, wondering how she could skirt the issue without telling a complete untruth.

"I'd offer to break it down, but the maintenance department wouldn't be too happy."

"Oh, no. That isn't necessary," she hastened to reassure him, aware that with his physique he probably could. "We have everything under control. It's nothing we can't handle," she added, glancing at the two women on either side of her—her nurse, forty-five-year-old Lynette Hayes, and Casey Owens's mother, Jill. She'd hoped they would nod in agreement, but both women wore distinct we-need-help expressions that Galen would have had to be blind not to notice.

"There are other facilities to use," he commented, his chocolate-brown eyes twinkling with merriment. "I know you've only been at Hope for a few days and probably don't know your way around, but this wing has two other restrooms."

Nikki braced herself against the warm feeling his dark gaze had once again created in her chest. She simply would *not* allow herself to fall back into old habits of imagining the impossible. He hadn't wanted her then, so she wouldn't foolishly think that he would want her now, no matter how engaging he was. They'd been friends and he hadn't wanted to change that.

"I'll make a point to check them out," she commented. "Now, I'm sure you have things to do and people to see, so don't let us keep you."

"You're not," he answered with the boyish grin that charmed his women patients and made it difficult for those in the grandparent generation to believe he was a highly skilled and experienced physician. "I was coming to visit you."

"Me?" What rotten luck, she thought as she toyed with the hairpin. "What for?"

"Lunch. For old times' sake?"

"I'm busy."

"Breaking into the restroom?"

She heaved a sigh. So much for secrecy. From the curiosity in his eyes, he wouldn't leave until he knew exactly what was going on. "If you must know," she said a trifle crossly, "a six-year-old has barricaded himself inside."

"A patient?"

"Yes."

"What's wrong with him?"

Mrs Owens answered. "A sore throat."

"Strep?" he asked Nikki.

Nikki shrugged. "I can't say for sure. He took off before I could examine him."

Galen's grin widened and a familiar impish sparkle appeared in his eyes. "My, my. Two days on the job and you've already earned an unsavory reputation with the young crowd, Dr Lawrence."

Nikki opened her mouth to protest, but Lynette broke in.

"It's my fault," the nurse confessed. "He asked if he'd get a shot like the last time and I said that we'd have to see what the doctor said. Before I knew it, he jumped off the table, ran out of the room and down the hall, then locked himself in here.''

Galen laughed. ''There never was a dull moment around you, Nik. This is great.''

Nikki crossed her arms, irritated as much by his use of her nickname from their happier days together as by him finding their predicament so humorous. ''I beg to differ.''

''Sorry. I know it's not funny, but...'' He shrugged.

''I'm sure we'll laugh about this someday, but not now,'' Nikki told him.

''You're right.'' His grin disappeared. ''Have you tried a key?''

''If I had one, do you think I'd be trying the hairpin trick?'' She didn't wait for his reply before she added, ''We've been waiting for someone from Housekeeping or Maintenance to bring a master key, but either they're busy or they've forgotten.''

''How long has he been in there?''

She glanced at Lynette and Mrs Owens. ''Twenty minutes or so.''

''Have you tried talking him out?''

Nikki's tongue formed a sarcastic comment but, considering their audience, it wasn't appropriate for one physician to argue with another. Instead, she glared at him. ''We have. We *all* have.''

If that was Galen's best suggestion, she'd better get back to work. She bent down to try her hairpin in the lock again as she raised her voice to speak through the closed door.

''Casey? It's lunchtime. Would you like to come out and eat? The cafeteria is serving chicken nuggets today. Your mom says they're your favorite.''

His reply was hoarse, but adamant. ''Don't want any.''

''How about a nice cup of ice cream? Or a Popsicle?''

''No.''

"I'll bet you're getting thirsty for something cold," Nikki coaxed as she jiggled her pin and listened for a click.

"I can get my own drink." The sound of water running confirmed his statement.

Galen crouched beside her. "Have you done this hairpin thing before?"

"No," Nikki said, intent on her task. "But once, when my older brother, Derek, wouldn't stop tormenting my friend and me, we locked ourselves in his bedroom to teach him not to mess with us. Fifteen minutes later, he'd picked the lock with a hairpin and chased us out." She grinned, remembering. "The good thing was, he left us alone for the rest of the evening."

Thinking she'd turned the tumbler, she rattled the knob, but it still wouldn't turn. She muttered an unladylike "Damn" under her breath.

"This could take all day," he commented.

"I never said I was a locksmith," she reminded him. "For the record, though, you make a much better door than a window."

And, oh, what a fine door he was. Six feet tall, solid, and built to last.

Irritated by her own thoughts and aggravated by how easily they'd formed, she wiggled the hairpin with more force than necessary.

"Sorry." He straightened. "If Casey doesn't want an injection, did anyone consider promising that he wouldn't get one?"

Nikki shifted her gaze to meet his. "Now, why didn't we think of that?" she answered sarcastically. "Of course we did. He didn't buy it."

"Maybe he will if he hears it from me. One man to another."

She wanted to refuse, but her diplomatic efforts had

failed and it didn't appear as if picking the lock would succeed any time soon either. "Be my guest," she grudgingly conceded.

Galen knocked on the door. "Casey? I'm Dr Stafford. I understand you don't like shots."

"They hurt."

"Will you come out if I promise that none of us will give you one?"

"I like being in here."

Galen glanced at Nikki, then at Casey's mother, who shrugged.

"I'm sure you do," he said. "But your mother wants to go home and I don't think you want to spend the afternoon and evening by yourself."

For a few seconds silence reigned, as if Casey was digesting this information. "Are there strange noises here?" he finally asked cautiously.

"Lots of them," Galen said cheerfully. "Hospitals are noisy places because people work here all night. You'd sleep better at home in your own bed."

Another pause. "You promise I won't get a shot?"

Nikki interrupted with a whisper. "You don't know what's wrong with him. What if he's—?"

He cut her off. "If he can pull off this type of stunt, he can't be deathly ill."

Nikki conceded the point.

Galen flashed a thumbs-up at her before he addressed the door. "I'm positive, Casey. No shots."

"Cross your heart?"

"Cross my heart," Galen repeated.

Another pause. "OK," came the answer. "Hey, Mom. Did you know that if I stand on the sink on my tippy toes, I can touch the ceiling?"

A look of horror crossed Mrs Owens's face. "Dear Lord," she breathed.

"How big *is* this kid?" Nikki mumbled to Lynette.

"Definite basketball-player material," Lynette responded with a shrug.

"Provided he doesn't break his neck before then."

"Stay calm," Galen murmured, before he raised his voice. "Are you standing on the sink now?"

"Yeah. Hey, there's a little spider web in the corner. We have them at our house, too, don't we, Mama?"

Mrs Owens closed her eyes as if praying for strength.

"Forget the spider web," Galen said firmly. "I want you to get down before you fall."

"Do I have to? It's really neat up here."

"Yes!" Galen and Mrs Owens chimed in at the same time.

Casey sounded reluctant. "All right. I— Whoops…" His word ended in a scream, followed by a crash and an eerie silence.

Mrs Owens covered her mouth with both hands as her eyes widened with dismay. "Oh, no. He fell."

Success was now imperative and extremely urgent. Nikki wiggled the pin, hardly aware of the sheen of sweat dotting her brow.

"Come on, Nikki," Galen urged.

"I know. I'm trying."

Suddenly Casey howled, which, considering the alternative, was a more welcome sound. "Mama," he cried out.

Mrs Owens placed a palm against the door. "Mama's here, Casey," she crooned. "Can you open the door?"

"My arm hurts. And I'm *bleeding*." His wail grew in volume after that pronouncement.

"We'll have to break the door down," Galen said

grimly as he placed a hand on her shoulder in an obvious gesture to get her to move. "Step aside. We can't wait any longer."

Nikki ignored the strange sensation of heat to focus on her job. "Hold on. I might have it." She carefully turned the pin until she heard a faint but familiar click. She turned the knob with relief. "We're in."

Galen immediately pushed open the door to reveal the tow-headed youngster sitting on the floor, cradling his arm as blood from a gash under his chin ran down his green-striped T-shirt.

"Mama," he cried as his mother rushed to crouch beside him and enfold him in her arms.

"Oh, sweetie," she said, her voice choked. "You're going to be fine."

"Mama," he wailed louder as Nikki yanked a fistful of paper towel from the dispenser.

Galen accepted the compress she'd made and pressed it to the cut under Casey's chin. "Looks like he hit his chin on the trash can. He's lucky. It could have been worse."

Nikki eyed the distance. Three feet wasn't a lot, but it was enough. A patch of water in the sink, obviously a splash from when Casey had gotten himself a drink, had probably caused the daredevil-in-training's foot to slip. Somehow she suspected this young man would cause his parents many sleepless nights and turn their hair prematurely gray.

Galen picked the boy off the floor. "Come on, big guy. Let's go see what you did to yourself." He looked at Nikki. "My place or yours?"

"He's my patient. Take him to room three," Nikki directed.

"Suit yourself."

She led the entourage into the exam cubicle and quickly

donned a pair of gloves while Galen placed a sniveling Casey on the exam table.

"Let's take a look at your chin," she said kindly, tipping his head back and removing the compress while she tried to forget Galen's presence in the background. Blood welled in the inch-long gash and she quickly mopped away the excess with a thick square of gauze that Lynette supplied before the nurse busied herself taking his pulse and temperature.

"Will he need stitches?" Mrs Owens asked in a low voice.

"He could use a few," Nikki admitted. If she went with the traditional treatment, she'd be using several needles—one for the local anesthetic injection and one to actually sew the wound closed. Considering Casey's aversion to shots and the promise Galen had made, stitching his gash was not an option. At least, not an option if she wanted the boy to trust her the next time he needed medical attention. From what she'd seen so far of Casey's temperament, he would definitely be back.

"Oh, dear."

She quickly thought of an alternative. "There's a glue available that works quite well, especially on young children, but I don't know if…" She glanced at Galen, eyebrows raised.

He answered as if he'd read her mind. "We have it."

Another crisis averted, she thought as she turned back to her patient's mother and smiled. "He'll only have to hold still for about thirty seconds, long enough for me to apply the Dermabond to the skin."

Relief filled Mrs Owens's eyes. "Oh, thank goodness."

"The downside is that he may end up with a larger scar, but if he does, it won't be noticeable under his chin. The choice is yours."

"There isn't any doubt. The glue."

Nikki nodded to Lynette, who'd pushed a wheeled stainless-steel tray, which held more gauze, disinfectant and the wound glue, next to the bed.

"I'm going to clean your cut," she told the youngster, "and then I'm going to paste your skin back together so you'll stop bleeding."

His lower lip trembled. "Will it hurt?"

Nikki smiled. "It might tickle, but it won't hurt."

He leaned against his mother's chest, his small brow knitted as if bracing himself for the worst. A few minutes later, after being disinfected and Dermabonded, he was all smiles.

"I didn't feel a thing," he boasted.

Nikki smiled. "What did I tell you?"

"How long will it last?" Mrs Owens asked.

"The glue dries hard and will start flaking off in about a week, leaving healed skin behind," Nikki explained. "So you won't need to come back unless you notice a problem."

Mrs Owens appeared surprised. "Really?"

"Oh, yes. It's quite tough. They initially tested it on hockey players and if the glue can hold up under the abuse those guys take, it should hold up on Casey." Nikki addressed the youngster again. "Now, I want you to open your mouth so I can look at your throat."

His blue eyes widened and he glanced wildly around the room until his gaze landed on Galen. "No shots. He promised."

"No shots," Nikki repeated.

Casey opened his mouth and Nikki quickly saw the red patches at the back of his throat. Before he could argue, she quickly rolled a cotton swab over the area. "So we can test for strep," she told his mother before she handed it to Lynette. "We'll have the results before you leave."

"That fast?"

Nikki smiled. "It doesn't take long. I'm also relatively sure they'll be positive."

Mrs Owens frowned. "Does that mean…?" She glanced down at her son.

"We'll give a liquid antibiotic. He won't bounce back as quickly as he would if we chose the other treatment, but we'll do what we can to fight the infection." She bent to Casey's eye level. "How's the arm?"

"Hurts."

Nikki carefully examined his forearm, suspecting that it might be a severe sprain rather than a fracture. "I'm going to send you to Radiology so they can take pictures of your arm and wrist. Have you ever had your picture taken at the hospital before?"

He shook his head, dislodging a few tears in the process.

"These are special pictures that let us see inside you," Nikki said, almost surprised that this was the daredevil's first potentially broken bone. "And just like the pictures your mom and dad take, these won't hurt. Can you hold still so the lady in X-ray can take them?"

"Yeah."

"All right, then. Off you go. Would you like to walk or ride?"

His eyes brightened. "Ride."

"OK. One wheelchair coming right up."

Lynette disappeared, then reappeared with a wheelchair. The pain in his arm, chin, and throat plainly forgotten at the prospect of this next experience, Casey's eyes glittered with excitement.

As Lynette wheeled him down the hall, accompanied by his mother, Nikki heard him ask, "Can we go fast?"

She shook her head in amusement at Galen, who was leaning against the counter. "He's definitely pure boy."

"I also predict many more visits."

As he straightened and flashed his familiar lazy smile, awareness shimmied down her spine. He wasn't the first man to tower over her, but he was the only one who made her nerve endings dance with anticipation. It was mildly frustrating to realize that her response, not to mention his clean, woodsy aftershave, hadn't changed over time.

"I do, too. For a kid who worries about pain, he's certainly fearless," she said, determined to concentrate on her patient instead of Galen.

"Ah, but when you're seeking a thrill, the potential for pain is at the back of your mind. He'll learn."

"The hard way," she predicted.

"Probably. So what's your answer?"

Her mind drew a blank. "To what?"

"Lunch."

"Casey is my lunch date."

"You'll be finished with him in forty minutes, if that long. You're officially closed until one-thirty."

"How do you know?"

"I used to work in the MEC before I moved into the ER full time." He glanced at his watch. "I figure that gives us about forty-five minutes to run down to the cafeteria."

"I shouldn't…" she said slowly, tempted to accept and certain she'd be foolish if she did.

After that fateful night when she'd thrown herself at him, she'd tweaked her work routine to avoid the inevitable awkward encounters. It had been easy because of all the distractions associated with ending their residencies—upcoming exams, evaluations, job interviews, and patients.

The sheer size of St Luke's, where it was rumored that

a medical student had gone to Pathology with a specimen and had never been seen again, had also helped. Unfortunately, staying out of Galen's way at Hope would be a lot more difficult. Her job description included covering the minor emergency clinic to free the ER for true emergencies and acting as Galen's back-up whenever the ER became swamped. Yet, with conscious effort, she could manage to limit the time they spent together.

She *would*.

"Come on," he coaxed. "They're serving Philly steak sandwiches today, with lots of green peppers and mozzarella cheese. Exactly the way you liked them."

"You remember?" she asked, surprised.

"Why wouldn't I? I lost track of the number of times we stopped at the sub shop after our shift to eat. You never ordered anything else. So, what do you say?"

She still hesitated. "I should review my afternoon patients' charts."

"Thirty minutes," he wheedled. "Surely you can spare that much time."

"I really can't."

A thoughtful look crossed his face. "Still in your workaholic phase?"

Working extra-long hours during those last few weeks had been her salvation and he'd clearly not forgotten.

"Since when is being thorough a flaw?" she countered.

His careful study nearly caused her to fidget. "It isn't," he said, "but you don't need to prove yourself to anyone here. Your recommendations were faultless."

"And how would you know?"

He grinned. "I asked. And added a few of my own."

Nikki wondered what he'd told his superiors, but sometimes ignorance was bliss. "Good recommendations don't come by accident."

"True," he admitted. "But skipping lunch on your first real day on duty isn't smart. Don't you know that your body burns more calories during times of stress?"

She raised her chin defiantly. "Who said I was under stress?"

He arched one eyebrow in his you-can't-fool-me-because-I-know-better look. "Learning a new routine in a new facility, moving into new quarters, having your patient lock himself in the restroom, seeing old friends and re-membering old…times." He hesitated as he raised one eyebrow. "Aren't they stressful events?"

"Maybe a little," she grudgingly admitted.

"I rest my case."

"But—"

"You should also know that you should eat when the opportunity arises. Hope City Hospital may not be as large as St Luke's or have the daily volume, but there'll still be plenty of days when the aroma wafting out of the cafeteria will be the closest you'll come to food."

His gentle warning chipped away at her resolve until it began to waver.

"If it will make you feel better," he added, "I'll put a special note in your personnel file that you wanted to skip lunch out of dedication to duty, but I corrupted you. They'll understand."

His grin was wide and so full of boyish charm that she chuckled. He was still as persistent and as persuasive as ever, and clearly his knack was well known. Perhaps it would be best if she agreed. Once this luncheon date was behind them, he'd no doubt go his way and she could go hers. She may have to help him out in the ER when things got hairy but, in a small town like Hope, how often would he have more patients than he could handle on his own?

"All right. Thirty minutes."

"Good." He looked inordinately pleased with himself. "I'll see you in the cafeteria at twelve forty-five. If you're not there by twelve-fifty, I'm coming to get you."

"Don't worry, I'll be there," she said.

He gave her a jaunty salute, then disappeared down the hallway, whistling a jolly, but unrecognizable tune.

Nikki watched him go, wondering if she would be strong enough to avoid falling under his spell once again.

CHAPTER TWO

GALEN strolled back to the ER, cautiously optimistic. Actually, he was more than optimistic. He was *determined* to succeed at straightening out the problems between himself and Nikki, and he had his colleague, Jared Tremaine, to thank for inadvertently pushing him in this direction.

If Jared hadn't asked him to befriend Annie and if Galen hadn't admitted that, although he liked the paramedic, the sparks weren't there, he would never have reached this particular point in his life.

Immediately after that conversation, an image of Nikki Lawrence, with her tawny long hair, dark eyes and gentle smile, had popped into his head and refused to budge.

She was the real reason as to why, at thirty-one, he didn't have a wifely prospect in sight.

No one else compared to the woman who had made him laugh, made him angry, and made him think he could conquer the world singlehandedly. And from extensive first-hand experience, he knew that no one else had made him feel as if they could generate enough energy to blast a space shuttle into orbit.

When she'd tried to seduce him, he'd been pleasantly surprised and extremely willing, until his good sense had overridden his hormones.

They'd been together for their entire residency, although it hadn't been until their third year that Galen had become aware of her as a woman rather than a fellow student and colleague. He could have acted on his impulses, but he'd been afraid to ruin the one constant in his life—Nikki's friendship.

He might have risked it if his friendship with her cousin Calvin hadn't also been at stake. Cal had been a college roommate and their friendship had flourished in spite of them being complete opposites, with Galen being the more daring of the two.

Cal had moved into geology while he'd pursued medicine, but they still stayed in contact. When he'd been accepted to St Luke's for his residency in emergency medicine, Cal had immediately informed him that his cousin Nikki had been selected as well. Her brothers had subsequently asked, via Cal, if Galen would mind steering her away from any unsavory characters who might take advantage of her sensitive nature. He hadn't wanted the job, but hadn't been able to refuse.

Over time, he got to know her and it became obvious that she was someone who deserved a man capable of giving her promises and white picket fences, not someone like him who didn't want anything more than a one-or two-night stand.

After his father had deserted them when he was six and his only sister ran away ten years later, he simply hadn't been interested in making promises, especially ones that he felt were highly unlikely to be kept—like love, honor, and cherish until death do us part—which was why he didn't date anyone more than a handful of times.

All of which made it impossible to have an affair with Nikki because it would have lumped him in the same category of unscrupulous jerks he was supposed to guard her against.

At odd moments, though, he imagined what it would be like if he *was* the guy she was meant to have, but he knew himself well enough to know that he couldn't give her the emotional ties she required any more than he could perform brain surgery. Like it or not, he was his father's son. His mother had always reminded him of how handsome he'd become, just like his father, but in Galen's mind, he'd feared that their similarities were more than skin-deep.

But he'd changed this past year—more specifically, the past six months. He'd grown weary of the dating scene and was finally willing to risk going after something more permanent. The problem was, the only woman he truly wanted was Nikki. As a locum who traveled extensively, she was nearly impossible to reach.

Before he could plan a strategy, Hope City Hospital landed in dire straits and fate offered a helping hand. They needed a temporary ER physician while Jared recovered from his injuries in the plane crash that had hurt two others and killed one.

He pulled as many strings as he could with his own administration to contact Nikki's agency, although he knew their chances of contracting her were slim. Locums were in great demand and their facility too desperate to be choosy. Yet it didn't stop him from taking the precaution of leaving his name out of the negotiations. If she still harbored hard feelings toward him, he didn't want to give her any grounds to refuse.

He'd never been more relieved than when they received the official word. Nikki was coming.

This time he hoped their story would have a different ending. With both of them living in a town with the same name, how could it be otherwise?

"What's going to be different?" Fern Pyle, an experienced ER nurse in her fifties, fell into step beside him.

Dragged out of his thoughts, Galen smoothly shifted gears. "Nothing. Just talking to myself."

"You're too young to start doing that," she teased.

"Age is just a state of mind."

"In that case, I'm definitely too old to be working here," she retorted. "I came to tell you that an entire family of six with severe gastroenteritis has arrived."

"Let me guess. They went to a picnic at the park."

"You're close. It was a family reunion."

He groaned. "How many attended this reunion?"

"I didn't ask."

He heaved a sigh. Six could easily become five times that number. His luncheon plans faded around the edges. "Ah, the joys of summer. 'Tis the season for food poisoning."

"Yeah, well, we're also getting a possible drug overdose and a broken collarbone, both by ambulance. ETA is ten minutes. Tops."

He shook his head. "I can't leave you guys alone for a minute. The ER was quiet before I went to the MEC."

Fern shrugged. "What can I say? It's the nature of the beast. Can you handle everyone or do you want us to call for back-up?"

The drug overdose was the most pressing and had the greatest potential for demanding a physician's sole attention. His plans for a quiet lunch in the cafeteria completely disappeared.

"Call Nik, er, Dr Lawrence," he said. "She can handle the collarbone after she finishes with her patient in the MEC."

"And the family?"

"They'll have to wait for whoever becomes available first."

Fern sped off toward the phone on the nurses' desk, but Galen stopped her. "Pick up two Philly steak sandwiches from the cafeteria for me, would you?"

"Two?"

"Two," he stated.

"Starving, are you?"

He grinned. "Always."

She glanced at her watch. "They usually run out by now."

"Try."

"OK," she said, sounding doubtful. "But do you really think you'll have time to eat?"

He grinned. Lunch had been merely an excuse to be with Nikki and as long as that happened, he didn't care what he ate, or when. "I'll make time," he said firmly. "A person should never neglect what's important."

Nikki sent Casey Owens and his mother on their way, glad that the rest of their visit had passed uneventfully. He'd suffered a buckle fracture, not a sprain as she'd suspected, so Nikki had put a cast on his arm and told them to return in six weeks. Wryly, she wished her next encounter with Galen was six weeks from now, rather than fifteen minutes.

If only she didn't remember that night as if it had happened yesterday…

She'd been studying hard and feeling overwhelmed as she'd reviewed notes that had suddenly seemed as if she'd never seen them before. The more tired she'd become, the more frantic she'd felt until Galen had walked into her apartment. She'd poured out her fears and he'd tried to comfort and encourage her, but she'd realized in the middle of his consoling hug that their careers would soon take them in different directions. They'd end up exchanging letters, phone calls and emails until eventually the busyness of their separate lives would send their friendship into the mists of memory.

The time to reveal her feelings for him had come. She simply hadn't been able to pass up this opportunity.

She'd tugged his shirt out of his pants and proceeded to pour out her years of loving him into a single kiss. He'd been more than willing until they'd shed nearly all their clothes. Then, without warning, he'd called an abrupt halt.

She was using him, he told her—using him as a means to temporarily forget her insecurities. He couldn't take what she offered when she wasn't thinking clearly.

He also went on to spout something about honor and promises made to her cousin, but she'd stopped listening. She'd never felt more exposed, both emotionally and physically, as she did at that moment.

After he slipped away, the shame of what she'd done, what she'd attempted to do, subsequently ruined their friendship. Oh, they apologized to each other and on the surface, acted as if the incident had never happened, but pretending didn't take away her embarrassment or boost her self-esteem.

To her relief…and sorrow…she left St Luke's with Galen's good luck wishes ringing in her ears.

Now they were together again.

The pager in her pocket bleeped with a message summoning her to the ER. She wondered if this was Galen's way of reminding her about lunch, but as soon as she crossed the threshold and saw the activity, she knew this wasn't a social call.

She headed for the trauma room that Fern had indicated with a curt "Room Two." Before she could enter, a pretty paramedic—A. McCall, according to her name tag—stopped her.

"Could I talk to you before you go in?" she asked Nikki in a low voice. "It's important."

Curious, Nikki nodded. As soon as they were out of earshot of the man waiting for attention, who probably couldn't have heard them anyway because of his demands for a painkiller, the young woman spoke.

"I just thought I'd warn you," she said. "This guy is a druggie, looking for a fix."

Nikki heard the man's demands grow louder. "You're sure?"

"Positive. I learned the hard way," she said ruefully. "He has a number of aliases and the last time I brought him in, as soon as my injection took hold he disappeared. Jared…" she colored slightly "…er, Dr Tremaine wasn't happy with me."

Nikki smiled. "I can imagine. But you're sure this is the same fellow?"

"Absolutely, right down to the birthmark on the side of his neck. Mr Johnson, or at least that's the name he's using today, can dislocate his shoulder at will. He's quite good at it."

Nikki had run across these people before. They tried their tricks until the staff caught onto their game, then skipped town to scam the unsuspecting staff at the next clinic or hospital.

"Thanks for the tip." Nikki eyed her nametag. "Ms McCall."

"Annie," the woman corrected as she shook Nikki's hand.

"Thanks, Annie. But if you gave him a shot before, how did you avoid giving him one this time?"

Annie smiled. "I didn't. I used saline. It worked until we drove up and then he started complaining because it hadn't kicked in yet. I told him that I didn't dare administer anything stronger because he'd already received the maximum dose."

"Did he believe you?"

She shrugged. "There wasn't much he could do."

"Well, thanks again. I'll take it from here."

Nikki walked into the exam room and greeted the blond twenty-five-year-old who was cradling his right arm. "So you dislocated your shoulder, Mr Johnson," she said calmly.

"Yes, and it's killing me."

"I'll be happy to give you something," she said, "but first we need X-rays."

He frowned. "X-rays?"

"Oh, yes. That doesn't appear to be a simple dislocation." She felt for the pulse in his wrist. It was steady and strong, but he didn't need to know that.

"I can tell from your pulse that you're losing circulation. We may have to call in an orthopedic consult." Nikki wrote a note and handed it to Ravi Kedar. "Would you please make the arrangements?"

The nurse accepted the note with a puzzled frown, read it, then slowly nodded. "Right away, Doctor."

"Good." Nikki turned back to her patient. "Now, let's hear the real story."

"I already told the ambulance people what happened."

"What time did you fall off the ladder?"

"I dunno. An hour ago."

"I don't think so." She straightened to her full five-foot four-inch height. "I might look like I'm naïve, but I'm not. Your injury didn't occur an hour ago. Your name is on our list, buddy."

"I don't know what you're talking about."

"Bluster all you want," she said bluntly. "You're addicted and you need help. I can get you in a drug rehab program within two hours—"

He jumped off the bed, his face twisted with fury. "Forget it."

"You need help."

"Yeah. I got plenty of help from you guys," he sneered. "It was one of you who got me hooked in the first place. If he'd fixed my shoulder the first time, I wouldn't have had to rely on medication."

"It started with a prescription?" Unfortunately, it did happen and for various reasons, but situations like Johnson's were sloppy mistakes on the part of uncaring physicians.

"Yeah." He glanced around the room. "Where did the other guy go?"

"To call Security."

He didn't waste a minute. He maneuvered his own arm until the bone slid back into place, then hopped off the bed as he stripped the pulse oximeter off one finger and the blood-pressure cuff from his arm. "Sorry, lady, but I ain't staying for whatever party you're planning."

She blocked his path, aware that her small frame didn't stand a chance. He wasn't that much larger, but addicts in need of a fix often found superhuman strength. "We can help you."

"Move outa my way," he ordered.

She didn't budge. "Give us a chance. You don't want to spend the rest of your life like this, do you? Going from place to place, trying to satisfy your craving?"

Suddenly he shoved her away as effortlessly as he would have a fly, then dashed out of the room.

Nikki slammed into the nearby tray table and sent everything on it crashing to the floor before she landed in the middle of the mess.

"What in the—?" Galen rushed in, followed by a worried Ravi and a pole-thin security guard, and helped her to her feet. "Are you hurt?"

"I'm fine," she said, before she looked past his shoulder to Ravi and the guard. "If you hurry, you might catch him outside. About five-seven, one-sixty, and chin-length blond hair."

The uniformed guard took off.

"Will someone tell me what's going on in my own ER?" Galen roared.

"I had a patient who decided to discharge himself AMA. Against medical advice," she added.

"I know what AMA means," he said grimly. "But that doesn't explain why you're on the floor and Neil is chasing after him."

"He didn't like my suggestion to check into a drug program. He chose to leave rather hurriedly instead."

"And you tried to stop him, I suppose."

She looked at him with affront. "Someone had to make him think about what he was doing and where his life was going. I couldn't let him just walk out of here."

"So he knocked you down and still walked out of here." A muscle in his jaw tensed.

"No," she corrected. "He ran."

"Who was he?"

"He went by Jake Johnson, but I understand he uses several names."

Galen nodded grimly. "We've met." He glanced at Ravi. "If he shows up ever again, notify Security immediately. No questions asked. Do I make myself clear?"

Ravi bobbed his head, his dark eyes wide. "Yes, sir."

"And make sure everyone else knows, too. I won't have this happening again."

"Yes, sir. I'll let everyone know."

"And you, Nikki," he faced her, "are going to file assault charges."

"Oh, for heaven's sake, Galen. If I hadn't stood in his way, he wouldn't have touched me."

"And what in heaven's name did you think you were

doing?'' he railed. ''You're no bigger than a minute, anyway. You're lucky he didn't throw you across the room. You might have broken your neck.''

Nikki bristled. Her height was her proverbial sore spot. Not that she cared about being shorter than nearly everyone else. It was strictly because too many people associated competence with being tall. Her stature had given her six-foot-five-inch brothers all the excuse they'd needed to be over-protective of their baby sister.

''My size doesn't affect my job performance or my brain power. I don't need to be over six feet tall like you and bench-press a hundred pounds in order to treat patients.''

''No, but there are times when muscles come in handy.''

''Today wasn't one of them.''

The guard returned. ''Sorry, Dr Lawrence. Your fellow vanished.''

''Somehow I'm not surprised,'' she said wryly. She reached down to pick the clipboard off the floor and dropped it again as her wrist protested.

''You *are* hurt.'' Galen grabbed her arm and began running his fingers over the skin, probing, prodding, then finally soothing.

Every nerve ending tingled under his tender touch and the rest of her body awakened from its year-long sleep. His fingertips generated sparks that swiftly flared into a bonfire. His scent completely surrounded her as the sleeve of his scrub shirt brushed against bare arm and she closed her eyes in something akin to pure joy.

Her good sense suddenly surfaced and she stiffened. No, she told herself. He was only being kind. His concern was no different than if she'd been any other colleague or staff member. She simply couldn't let Galen know that he still possessed the power to make her knees weak and her toes curl. He might be a great doctor and a friend who'd give her the shirt off his back if necessary, but he wasn't the kind of man she should be interested in. His father's abandonment and his younger sister's disappearance had scarred him to the place where he equated commitment with a noose around his neck.

She jerked her hand out of his grasp. "It's fine," she insisted sharply. "Bruised, but not broken."

"You should have an X-ray."

"Absolutely not. I refuse to get caught up in the paperwork over nothing. Now, did you come in here to be nosy or did you want to ask me a question?"

He frowned as if he hated to let the current subject drop but knew he had no choice in the matter. "I'd like a second opinion. My patient is comatose, with no visible reason for it."

"There has to be a reason, Galen," she said, realizing how easily his name had rolled off her tongue. "It isn't normal to be unconscious."

"You're not telling me anything I don't already know," he said dryly as he led her to the next cubicle. "I'm afraid I'm missing something, so I want you to look at him and tell me what you think."

Nikki approached the bed, noting the airway and IV in the man with distinct Asian features. A quick glance showed a fairly normal heart rhythm, although the rate was depressed and his blood pressure was low.

"What's the story?" she asked.

"The hotel maid found him this morning when she went to clean his room. At first she thought he was sleeping, but as the day went on she noticed he hadn't moved a muscle. She tried to rouse him and couldn't, so the manager called 911. At first the paramedics thought it was a drug overdose, but they couldn't find any pills in the room.''

''Do we have a name?''

''He's registered as a Michael Kwan. The EMS folks didn't wait around for more information. The cops are supposedly going through his hotel room looking for his driver's license. Before you ask, they didn't find any prescription bottles lying around either.''

By rote, she ran through the simple pneumonic for the causes of unconsciousness: AEIOU TIPS.

''His alcohol level is zero and his glucose is normal,'' Galen supplied, as if he'd read her mind.

She mentally checked off ''A'' for alcohol and ''I'' for insulin and went back to ''E''. ''Epilepsy? Anything in the environment?''

He shook his head. ''No signs of seizure and it was a standard hotel room. No chemicals.''

''And you're positive it isn't an overdose?''

''Toxicology results aren't completed yet, but we haven't found any needle tracks and none of our antidotes, especially Narcan, have had any effect.''

Next on the list was ''U''. ''Uremia?''

He handed over the preliminary lab report. ''Everything's out of whack, but nothing that would explain being unconscious.''

She moved on to the TIPS. ''No visible signs of trauma?''

''None.''

''No infection either,'' she mused aloud, noting the normal white-blood count.

''I ordered a blood culture anyway,'' he said. ''It'll take about six hours for a preliminary, but I doubt if it will grow any of the usual bugs.''

''Have you thought of a psychiatric consult?''

"If all else fails. It could be a stroke."

"It's possible." She began her own examination. "Pupils are fixed and dilated. He's been sick for some time, I'd say. He's pale and has poor muscle tone. And see how baggy his clothes are? He's recently lost weight."

She straightened, running through her options. "I'd bet something's going on upstairs." She tapped her forehead. "We'd better get a CT scan."

"Mr Kwan is next in line," he told her.

"Then I'd say you've covered all your bases."

Kwan's turn for a CT scan arrived a few minutes later. Before the radiologist reported a brain tumor near his brain stem, the lab called with the rest of the toxicology findings. Their patient had ingested a large amount of acetominophen, but whether it had been by choice or by accident to control an uncontrollable headache, no one would know. In any case, it was a moot point. He had been dying by inches and trying to counteract his overdose wouldn't affect his outcome. All they could do was to make him comfortable.

His breathing gradually became more depressed and Nikki knew his time was short.

"You don't need to stay," Galen told her as he dashed in to check on him in between attending to his family with the intestinal complaints.

"Yes, I do," she said. "When the police find his family, I want to reassure them that their husband or father or son didn't spend his final moments alone."

He nodded, then left as soundlessly as he'd arrived.

Nikki watched over Mr Kwan, imagining all sorts of scenarios as to how and why he'd ended up in the town of Hope at this stage in his life. He had to have known about his tumor: its size was such that he would definitely have had signs and symptoms of its presence.

Had he come to Hope in search of a miracle, or simply to find closure in the same way that she had?

Her assignment to a town whose name encouraged looking to the future and not the past had appeared like a gift from heaven. She'd been weary of catching herself watching for Galen and seeing him in every tall, brown-haired man who'd crossed her path and so she'd given herself an ultimatum to stop. It had been time to fill the void in her heart with something more personal than her career.

How ironic to find the man who'd created that void in this very place.

Her patient interrupted her thoughts with a final shuddering gasp. The end had come quite peacefully. The knowledge would provide some consolation to his family, if he even had family.

She shut off the monitors, closed his eyes, drew the sheet over his face, and strode from the room.

Galen caught her before she turned down the hallway leading to her own clinic. "Are you OK?"

"Yeah," she answered. "It's just a shame he was a long way from home. Have the police called?"

"The last I heard, they're still working on tracking down his next of kin." He paused. "I tried to grab us a few sandwiches to eat on the run, but the cafeteria had sold out."

"That's OK. I don't usually eat lunch anyway."

"Then how about dinner? At eight?"

"I'm still unpacking."

"All the more reason to go out."

"Not tonight," she said firmly.

"OK," he said, as if he'd realized that she wouldn't be persuaded. "What do you say to later in the week?"

She was too tired to argue. "Maybe."

"Friday it is," he answered as if she'd said yes. Before

she could object, he added, ''Thanks for your help. If I can ever repay the favor, I'm only a phone call away.''

''I'm sure I'll manage on my own,'' she said, determined not to ask for his assistance unless absolutely necessary. After working in hospitals where she saw more emergencies in a single shift than Hope would see in a week, handling a minor emergency center and walk-in medical clinic would be a breeze.

''I'm sure you can, but technically we're supposed to be here for each other.''

Her heart skipped a beat as she tried not to read more into his comment than necessary.

''Nikki...'' he began.

His tone suggested that he was going to touch on a subject that was best left forgotten. She braced herself. ''Yes?''

''Do you ever wonder what would have happened if we'd made love that night?'' he asked softly, his gaze intent.

All the time.

She couldn't say that, however, so she hid behind a carefree attitude. ''Why would I do that?'' she prevaricated.

''Because it's been at the back of our minds for the past year,'' he said. ''We need to finally get everything out in the open.''

She waved aside his suggestion. ''For heaven's sake, Galen, why? There's nothing to discuss. In fact, I can barely remember what happened.''

Liar, her little voice screamed at her.

His eyes gleamed with something she couldn't quite identify. ''Fool yourself all you want, Nikki, but you haven't forgotten a single minute. Neither have I.''

She broke eye contact, certain he would see more than

she wanted him to. It didn't seem fair that he could read her so easily when he hadn't done so before.

"Maybe not," she admitted slowly, "but talking didn't change the outcome back then and it won't change it now, so let's drop the subject, once and for all."

His gaze grew intent. "I can't do that, Nik."

If she'd learned one thing about Galen during their residency, it had been that he was persistent when he felt strongly about something. She could either give in or wait for him to wear her down like water dripping on a stone, but in the end he would get his way. She'd prefer to have it happen on her terms and not his.

"OK, but you said yourself that moving to a new town and learning a new routine was stressful. Can we wait a while before we take our trip down memory lane?"

He nodded once. "OK. We'll wait. But not for long."

Now that Nikki was here, Galen wanted to clear the air as quickly as possible. They'd already wasted an entire year, but she'd be living in Hope for at least two months so he could afford to give her enough time to settle into her new routine.

He'd hold off for a week and not one day longer.

Meanwhile, if she thought she could avoid him, she could think again. He might have been willing to keep a low profile during this seven-day reprieve, but he'd seen her reaction when he'd checked her bruised arm. She hadn't shivered because she'd been cold—she'd shivered because she'd felt something in his touch. She clearly wasn't as unmoved as she pretended to be and he intended to take advantage of that observation, even to the point of visiting her, uninvited.

Whether she liked it or not, whether she wanted it or

not, he was determined to make himself an integral part of her life, to show her that he'd changed his priorities.

The address he'd wangled out of the clerk in Personnel had listed her apartment as 3D. He wasn't surprised she'd taken the uppermost floor. Nikki's favorite spot at St Luke's had been on the roof or, in case of bad weather, the lounge on the fifteenth floor that provided the best view of the city.

Too impatient for the elevator, he took the stairs two at a time, but she didn't answer her doorbell.

He could wait, he supposed, but it might take hours until she returned. Just because a Toyota with an out-of-state license plate was parked in her space, it didn't mean she was at home. Lots of things—a grocery story, the city park, a diner—were within walking distance.

Disappointed, he returned to the ground floor. On the odd chance that she'd been sitting on her balcony and couldn't hear the bell, he walked around the building. To his delight, he saw her through the wrought-iron railing, relaxing on a lawn chair, eyes closed.

Without hesitation, he selected a pebble from someone's rock garden, and wound up with his best pitch. The small stone clanged against the railing and she opened her eyes to glance down.

Galen waved. ''Hi.''

''Speak of the devil,'' she told him wryly. ''What are you doing here?''

''To see you.''

''What for?''

He thought fast for a plausible excuse. ''To check your arm.''

''It's fine.''

''I want to make sure.''

"Take my word for it. Don't you have a hot date or something?"

"Nope."

"A pity."

He quickly ignored her sarcasm and thought of another excuse. "I also thought you might like to hear about Mr Kwan."

"You could tell me tomorrow."

"You're right. I could." He turned to leave, hoping he'd sparked her curiosity.

"Wait," she called, rising to stand at the railing. "Did the police find his family?"

He stopped, hiding his relief that she'd nibbled at his bait. "Shall we discuss this privately, or do you want everyone in the complex to hear our conversation?"

She worried her bottom lip with her teeth before she straightened. "All right. Come on up."

The battle had begun.

CHAPTER THREE

NIKKI watched Galen disappear around the corner and nibbled on her lip in indecision. If another colleague had dropped by, she would have invited him into her apartment without hesitation, so why couldn't she do the same with Galen?

Because if he'd stayed out of sight, he'd stay out of her mind, she admitted. He obviously knew that, too, which probably explained why he'd showed up on such a flimsy excuse. Check her arm, indeed! If she couldn't treat a slight sprain, then a medical refresher course was in order.

Lucky for him that she was curious about Mr Kwan, otherwise he'd be on his way home at this very moment.

Instinctively, she knew that he wouldn't let her avoid him as easily as she had at St Luke's. After two short days, she'd already learned that the lines separating their departments existed only on paper. For all intents and purposes, she was simply another branch of the ER and could expect to see him more often than not.

With that standard operating procedure in place, someone in the hospital would notice if she balked at the idea or steered clear of him. He or she would speculate why, another would add his or her opinion, and before she could say "Code Blue," the grapevine would buzz with a story more sensational than the latest movie of the week. Heaven help her if they stumbled onto the truth.

She simply had to make the best of an uncomfortable situation. She didn't have a choice.

Resigned to the inevitable, she flung open her door just

as he raised his hand to knock. "You're fast," she commented as she stepped aside so he could enter.

"Only when it counts," he answered with a grin.

"So tell me about Mr Kwan," she said as she led him into the living room.

"Come on, Nik. What sort of hospitality are you giving these days?" he protested good-naturedly. "I remember being handed a bottle of beer or a soda as soon as I walked in."

"If I'd known you were coming, I would have stocked up on Dr Pepper," she said, referring to his favorite soft drink, "but I didn't, so you have to choose between cherry cola and water."

"Cherry cola."

She walked into her small kitchen, suddenly conscious of him following her. Galen's sheer size made the walls move in closer until she thought she couldn't turn from the counter to the refrigerator and back again without bumping into him.

"Would you like to sit in the living room or on the balcony?" she asked as she prepared a glass filled with lots of soda and little ice, just the way he liked it.

"Wherever you're most comfortable," he answered promptly, although he didn't budge from leaning against the breakfast bar. "Remember when we'd sit on the roof near the helipad during our lunch-break and watch the people below run around like ants?"

Nikki saw through his ploy, but because it seemed so reminiscent of old times when they'd discussed their days and shared their experiences, and because she did miss "the good ole days" even though they hadn't been that long ago, she generously decided to give him some leeway.

"We did our own share of running when a chopper was

coming in,'' she said dryly. ''The roof was the best place to get away and still be close enough if we were paged.''

''It was,'' he agreed. ''And remember all the times we took late supper breaks so we could sit in the tenth-floor lounge to stare at the skyline and watch the city light up?''

She smiled without any effort. ''It was a great place to go and think. As I recall, you liked the lounge better than the rooftop.''

He shrugged. ''Only because I didn't have to worry about accidentally falling over the edge. But you're right. Both places were great ten-minute getaways.''

He fell silent and his gaze grew intent. ''I looked for you there during those last few weeks,'' he said quietly. ''I thought I'd eventually run into you.''

She ran a finger through the condensation on her glass before she answered. ''I was too busy. We both were.''

Her excuse was only partly true. Because she'd held a lot of fond memories of their common meeting place, she'd purposely stayed away. There simply hadn't been any point in rubbing salt into an open wound. She'd assumed that he wouldn't try to find her, but knowing that he had purposely sought her out gave her an odd feeling.

''Yeah, we were.'' To her relief, he didn't go further but instead pointed to her glass balcony door. ''With your penchant for high places, I'm not surprised you chose the top-floor apartment.''

She shrugged. ''What can I say? There's something powerful about being high enough to touch the clouds and breathe the air before someone else has.''

''The little bird imagines she's an eagle.''

''It's easier to think when you're away from the crowd,'' she corrected. ''Fewer distractions.''

''And you can look down at people instead of up.''

"That, too." She motioned toward the living room. "Shall we?"

He chose an oversized chair while she sank onto the striped sofa. "I recognize the afghan, but not the furniture," he said.

She stroked the brightly colored woven throw. That rectangle of soft fabric had dried a lot of tears and heard a lot of heartfelt thoughts. Thank goodness it couldn't talk!

"The apartment came fully furnished," she explained. "It's too difficult to move sofas and chairs and tables every few weeks or months, so I don't. My things are in Blue Springs, gathering dust in my condominium."

"Then you don't go home often?"

"I usually spend a week or two there in between jobs. Sometimes, if I get a long weekend, I'll drive back, but I usually stay at my current assignment for the duration."

Now, why did you tell him that? she mentally scolded herself. *Outlining your routine isn't the way to maintain distance.*

She steered the conversation in another direction. "What's the story on Mr Kwan?"

"Impatient, are we?"

"It's why you came, isn't it?"

"Not entirely," he corrected. "Your arm, remember?"

She held it out and flexed her fingers. "It's fine. See? Now, about Mr Kwan…"

Another lazy grin appeared, as if he wanted to delay again, but he didn't. "Apparently, he's recently divorced. His ex didn't know anything about his health and was quite shocked to hear of his death. She gave me the name of his physician and when I spoke to him, he said that Kwan canceled every one of his scheduled oncology appointments."

"Then he wanted to die."

''One would think that,'' he said. ''Which is a shame because he was supposedly a computer genius. Anyway, they're shipping his body back to St Louis. It's a sad state of affairs, but unfortunately life doesn't always turn out the way we'd like.''

''I'll second that,'' she said fervently, thinking of her own disappointments.

''How's your family?'' he asked, clearly changing the subject to one more upbeat. ''Are your brothers still keeping close tabs on you?''

Thinking of her five older siblings, she smiled fondly. ''Yes and no. They've learned that I'm hard to catch, even with a cellphone, so each week I call one of them instead of vice versa. We visit and the lucky one passes the word along to the others. This week is Derek's turn.''

''And they're satisfied with this arrangement?''

She laughed, well aware of how over-protective they were. ''Not really, but after I stopped answering the phone when I saw their numbers on my caller ID, they realized I meant business. I may be their baby sister and a foot shorter than the smallest of them, but I've also grown up.''

''Did you know I was jealous of you?'' he asked off-handedly.

''No,'' she said slowly, surprised by his confession. ''I didn't.''

''I always felt like I was on the outside of a group, looking in. Did you know that was one of the reasons why I agreed to keep a watchful eye on you when Cal asked? It made me feel as if I were a part of your family.''

''I never knew... Even when you joined us for holidays, I never knew...''

He shrugged. ''You weren't supposed to.''

Obviously, she hadn't been the only one hiding her innermost thoughts. "I assume you never heard from your sister?"

"Not a word. With Mom gone, Mary wouldn't be able to contact me even if she wanted to."

She wanted to touch him and offer her sympathy. He might act as if the situation didn't bother him, but she knew better. "Why not?"

"Few people in our home town know that I'm living in Hope." His eyes brightened. "Isn't it funny how things worked out? You were the one who seemed most suited to settling in one place and now you're traveling around the country, while I, who don't have any roots at all, have planted them."

"It is," she agreed. "I'm surprised you left Seattle. You couldn't wait to go there."

"It was a great place, but after seeing so much of the same thing we saw during our training—knifings, gunshot wounds, assaults, and running full tilt—I thought I'd like a slower pace. I read about Hope City Hospital and it sounded like a nice, quiet place, so I thought, Why not?"

"And you were hired."

"Moved here last fall," he commented. "Aren't you still with the same agency?"

"Yes, but I almost changed jobs, too," she admitted. "My boss wasn't an easy man to work for. He was an older doctor who thought women should stick to obstetrics. He'd never give me long-term assignments, so I was constantly living out of my suitcase. By the time I'd decided to find something else, he'd sold the business, so I stayed to see if things improved. Fortunately for me, they did."

"But you still move around a lot."

"Yes, but I rarely go anywhere for less than a month. The most time I've spent in one place is eight weeks when I covered a woman's maternity leave."

"And now you're at Hope. It's quite a coincidence that we ended up in the same place."

Galen looked too innocent and his tone too light-hearted for her to believe that fate had taken complete charge. He'd known the name of her agency, so he'd clearly had an unfair advantage.

"Yes, isn't it?" she asked dryly. "In fact, I'd guess you're responsible for me being here, aren't you?"

He chuckled. "I had nothing to do with Hope City needing a locum. Jared's plane crash was beyond my control."

"I don't mean his accident," she said crossly. "I'm talking about selecting his replacement."

He shrugged. "I can't take all the credit. I only played a minor role."

"How minor is 'minor'?"

"I'd mentioned your agency to our CEO and he placed the call. When we visited with a representative, I mentioned that we'd prefer having you if it was possible, but we didn't cut any special deals or receive any promises. We knew we would get the first available ER physician. I just wanted him or her to be you and I was willing to nudge things in that direction."

Nikki suspected he'd done more than nudge, but it didn't change the fact that the final decision had been hers. Philip Barnes, her boss, might recommend a position or try to convince her take it, but if she refused to go, he didn't force her.

"When I'd heard that Hope had specifically requested me, it seemed odd because I'd never been here before and didn't know a soul on the staff. Now it makes sense."

Although she hadn't intended to touch upon their history and had planned to avoid it, curiosity made her ask, "Why did you care if I came or not?"

He raised one eyebrow. "I missed you."

"You had my phone number and email address."

He shook his head. "Not good enough."

"Why not?"

"Because you rarely returned my calls. I started to suspect it was because we didn't part on the best of terms."

She stiffened, suddenly realizing that he'd masterfully led her to the conversation she'd intended to avoid. "Yes, we did. I distinctly remember wishing you good luck."

"You said it like we were strangers. Not friends who'd seen each other through thick and thin. On those rare times since then when I've spoken with you, it was the same."

Clearly, he'd seen through her façade.

"We were drifting apart," she defended herself. "It was inevitable. In another year we'd exchange the obligatory Christmas card and that would be it."

"I thought we were headed in that direction," he said, nodding, "so I decided to chart an intercept course."

"*You* decided?" she sputtered. "Why did you care one way or another?"

"I just did," he said firmly. "You see, I started thinking about that night. At the time I understood your embarrassment and how we both had so much going on in our lives, but I thought the tension between us would blow over in the end."

"It did," she insisted.

"No, it didn't. Cal mentioned how you were working too hard and I began to ask myself why you hadn't eased up on yourself and why you weren't seeing anyone."

"I date," she protested. "Long-distance romances don't work, so I decided to take a page from the same relationship and dating manual you've been using. It's worked for you all this time. Why shouldn't it work for me?"

He continued as if she hadn't interrupted. "I was trying

to think of the best way to approach you when suddenly a golden opportunity fell into my lap. I grabbed it.''

"You should have let sleeping dogs lie.''

"I couldn't. I was wrong to let this much time go by without tackling the real issue.''

The real issue? Oh, dear. He suspected there was an issue? The best defense was a good offense, or so she'd learned during those years spent watching pro football with her brothers. She put the theory to the test.

"You should have been open and honest about being here,'' she told him. "I don't like being manipulated.''

"I didn't manipulate you. The choice to accept our position or not was always yours. I merely worked behind the scenes.''

"Exactly. Which is why you should have—''

He leaned forward to interrupt, his gaze intent. "Speaking of being open and honest, would you have come to Hope if you'd known I was on the staff?''

He'd backed her into the proverbial corner. If she said no, which is exactly what she would have done, he would demand an explanation. If she answered the opposite, she'd have to give a plausible excuse for why their foundation of friendship had crumbled. Even if she hadn't fallen in love with him, they'd shared so much and had grown so close because of their common experiences that they would never have become two people who only jotted a few lines to each other during the holidays.

Suddenly she was tired of the game. Once he knew the truth, he'd do the right thing and leave her alone.

"You're right,'' she said, unflinchingly meeting his gaze. "I wouldn't have come because of the way I felt. Being around you is too difficult.''

"Difficult? Did you hate me that much for being a voice of reason that night?''

"Hate you?" Her chuckle was forced. "Oh, I'd tried to. At the time I told myself that I did, but…" She paused and, suddenly unable to go on, turned to stare out the balcony door.

She sensed rather than saw him move behind her. "For the record, I didn't want to leave you." He spoke calmly over her shoulder. "I'd wanted to stay, more than you can imagine."

She whirled to face him as she snorted an unladylike snort. "You couldn't leave my apartment fast enough. Your tire tracks are probably still on the street."

"I was angry. And hurt."

"Hurt? Hah! You accused me of using you."

"Weren't you?"

"No!" She was aghast. "Never!"

"Can I help it if your timing was suspect?" he roared. "How was I supposed to know if sleeping together truly meant something to you? That it wasn't a fluke or something you'd eventually regret?"

Her emotions bubbled to the surface and she poked him in the chest with her fingernail. "Because I loved you, dammit! *You*!"

Nikki's words hung in the air like morning mist. *She'd loved him?*

At odd times over the past few months he'd thought it might be a possibility, but had refused to jump to any conclusions or raise false hopes.

He repeated the words aloud, both awed and pleased by her admission. "You love me?"

She squared her shoulders and looked away. "Loved. With a 'D'. Past tense."

Galen doubted if it was as far in the past as she tried to believe, otherwise she wouldn't have fought so hard to stay away from him. "You can't turn something like that on and off."

"Maybe not, but I've had a year to recover."

"For what it's worth, I'm sorry for not realizing how you felt before now."

"How could you? You were too busy dating every woman who smiled in your direction."

"I did not," he protested.

"Maybe not *every* one," she admitted. "Now that I think about it, there were a few others—the nurse with the crooked teeth, the pharmacy tech who had a bad case of acne, and—"

"Hey, I wasn't that shallow."

"No, but the fact is, you filled all the pages in your little black book. As for me, I did my best to hide my feelings, especially after I saw how you kissed that red-headed respiratory therapist goodnight. On a scale of ten, it ranked as a twelve."

"You were wrong," he protested. "I don't even remember who she was."

"Regardless, all you ever gave me were friendly pecks on New Year's Eve, Christmas, and my birthday."

"Because I didn't trust myself. I was afraid to ruin our friendship."

"Puhleeze." She rolled her eyes. "You obviously weren't worried about ruining any friendship with what's-her-name."

"I also hadn't promised her cousin that I'd watch out for her so she wouldn't hook up with the wrong guy."

"And I suppose *you* thought that you were the wrong guy."

"Yes," he said simply. "Someone had to keep you from making a mistake."

She poked a finger in his chest. "That's another thing.

It's bad enough my brothers still see me as their baby sister, but I expected better of you. After all we went through in the ER, all the cases we worked on, I can't believe that you felt you should make this decision for me. What hurt most of all was how you apparently thought I didn't know my own mind. You had no right to decide on who was good for me and who wasn't.''

''I made that promise to Cal when he realized we'd be in the same hospital.''

''You shouldn't have.''

''Maybe not, but I did save your pretty butt on a few occasions. Remember the biker fellow who thought he'd take you home on his Harley because you smiled at him after you stitched up his chest? He'd carried you halfway through the ER before I stopped him. And don't forget the paranoid schizophrenic who backed you into a corner because his voices were telling him to.''

''OK, OK. I'll admit you rode to my rescue a time or two. You would have done the same even if Cal hadn't asked.''

He met her gaze. ''Probably, but I rarely made promises and when I did, I intended to keep them. The point is, you should have given me some clues that you were interested. When things escalated without warning—''

''Oh yeah.'' Her sarcasm rang out loud and clear. ''What sort of clues did you want? We were together more than we were apart. When I finally showed you how I felt, you ran. Do you remember Serena?''

''Yeah.'' He answered cautiously.

''After you stopped seeing her, I started to think that if I played my cards right, you'd eventually notice me. Time after time, you latched onto someone else.''

''So that's why you always made snide remarks about the nurses I asked out.''

"Yeah, no matter what juicy tidbit I passed along, you didn't pay attention. And if I had spelled things out, would your reaction have been any different?"

Considering how he'd taken both his role of protector and his promise seriously, probably not. "I wanted you, too, but I was trying to be noble and trying to avoid giving your brothers or your cousin an excuse to rip my head off. I was Cal's friend and he knew me better than anyone. Chances were good that he wouldn't have been happy to welcome me into the family as more than an old buddy. And if he hadn't been happy, I can guarantee your brothers wouldn't have been either."

"I would have protected you," she said solemnly.

"Oh, yeah," he scoffed, envisioning a little chickadee guarding its mate from five—make that six—huge vultures. "They would have turned me into mincemeat."

"I would have," she insisted, "but whatever they would or wouldn't have done isn't important any more. We're two different people with different ideas and different feelings."

"Speak for yourself, Nikki. Why do you think I was so eager to see you again?"

"It's over, Galen." Her voice was flat. "We can't go back."

If Nikki had loved him during their years of residency, he couldn't imagine how she could write him off as a lost cause. Surely she still carried a seed of attraction—a seed that, if properly nourished, would grow. Unless…

"You don't believe me, do you?" he asked.

She fell silent. "Your claim is a little hard to swallow. We need to be on good terms for the next few weeks, but you don't have to whitewash the facts for my sake. I can handle the truth. You never thought of me as anything more than a friend you could count on when you needed one.''

He stood abruptly. ''What will it take for you to trust me? To believe I *am* telling you the truth about wanting you?''

She raised her shoulders helplessly. ''I don't know.''

''Well, I can think of one way.'' He began yanking at his shirt buttons, baring his chest while fixing his gaze on hers.

Her jaw dropped. ''What...what are you doing?''

''We're going to finish what we started a year ago. I tried to act honorably then, but this time there are only two of us in this room. Your brothers, your cousin and everyone else in your family isn't here. Just you and me, baby.''

She rose, her face turning a becoming shade of pink. ''You can't do this, Galen. It's...it's *crazy*.''

''No, it's not. It makes perfect sense,'' he said calmly as he released the last button and started toward her.

Nikki stared at Galen, hardly able to believe what was happening. He wore the look of determination of a conqueror, and he was headed straight for her.

She backed up a few steps, feeling a combination of wariness and excitement. ''Now, Galen, think about what you're doing. Nothing has changed.''

''*I've* changed, and I have thought about this. I want to finish what we started a year ago.''

''You can't.'' She still wanted him, heaven help her, but not like this, not without assurances of love or affection and certainly not to prove a point.

She backed up again, until the wall blocked her retreat. Before she could sidestep him, he trapped her in place.

His scent surrounded her and his bared chest was an

inch from hers. She sensed his frustration and anger, but he was still the man she remembered, the finest she'd ever known, and he would never, *ever* lose control.

"Galen?" Her voice quaked as she stared into his eyes and tried to read the message she found there.

His voice softened and the corners of his mouth turned into a gentle smile. "Don't be afraid."

She managed to swallow at the same time she willed her adrenalin back to normal levels. The combination of ninety per cent excitement and ten per cent alarm had made her heart pound. "I'm not."

"I'd never hurt you."

"I know." Whatever happened, whatever he planned for the next few minutes, he wouldn't do anything without her being a willing participant. Tentatively, she touched the side of his face.

His mouth settled over hers and the past faded into insignificance as she concentrated on the present and the delicious sensations he was creating inside her. Smoothly and without her consciously realizing how it had happened, she found herself locked in a bear hug of an embrace that she had no desire to escape.

She slipped her arms inside his open shirt and snaked them around his middle. He was warm and solid and simply perfect.

He immediately moved one leg between hers, pressing his full length against her frame. The hard ridge resting against her abdomen spoke more loudly and was more convincing than anything he might have said. It was all the evidence she needed that he'd been telling her truth.

He wanted her.

Not the parade of nurses, the sexy respiratory therapist, or the radiology tech. None of those women had mattered.

Or had they? An unwelcome thought burst through her

sensual haze—a thought that played on the insecurities still tethered to her self-esteem.

She pulled back.

''What's wrong?'' he asked.

''How long has it been?''

A puzzled furrow appeared on his brow. ''What are you talking about? How long has *what* been?''

''Do you want me because you want *me*,'' she asked bluntly, ''or because you've already dated every available woman in town and I'm fresh meat?''

''No. Absolutely not. Would I have gone to this much trouble to get you here if I simply wanted someone new to *date*?''

He sounded affronted and looked the part. As one of her old mentors had said repeatedly, ''If it looks like a duck and acts like a duck, it probably is…'' Unfortunately, old habits died hard.

She retreated another step because she couldn't think, standing this close to him. ''I want to believe you and I'm trying, but—''

He gave a long-suffering sigh. ''But you need more than a single kiss.''

She hesitated a fraction of a second. ''I know you, Galen. You've always shied away from commitment to a woman and you never denied it. You can't blame me if I find it difficult to believe that you've turned a hundred and eighty degrees in a year. You have a track record of becoming bored with a steady diet.''

''Hold onto your stethoscope, because I intend to prove otherwise.''

''Then you're saying that you're ready and willing to throw away your little black book for one woman? The same woman you knew for three years and let slip through your fingers?''

"I know it sounds far-fetched, but yes." He softened his tone. "I'm tired of not having roots to call my own and I'm tired of being alone."

"Which is all the more reason for you not to waste your time," she told him flatly. "I'm a locum, Galen. I'm gone for weeks at a time and I'm leaving Hope in two months. Even if you convinced me during that time, we'll still end up apart."

"We definitely will if we don't try. Come on, Nik," he urged. "We have everything to gain and nothing to lose."

She had plenty to lose, she wanted to cry out. At the top of the list was her heart.

"Hey, Nik, what's happening?"

Nikki smiled at her brother's lazy drawl as she leaned back in her desk chair on Friday afternoon and pictured him doing the same in his office. Derek was two years older than she was and a high-powered sales rep for sports equipment. He'd been the one most enamored by his little sister because her arrival had taken away his baby-of-the-family status and had made him feel grown up.

"Saving lives, as usual," she quipped.

"Still working twenty-hour days?"

She heard the worry underlying his innocent tone. "I'm in Hope, remember? If we count every man, woman, dog, and cat in the county, we might have a population of twenty thousand."

"Then you have a slower pace."

She thought of her morning. Ten walk-in patients with everything from migraine headaches to infected gashes. And that didn't include the car accident that had brought five kids and two adults to the hospital.

"To a certain degree," she admitted.

"That's good. You don't sound as stressed as you have

been. Everyone will be glad to hear you're turning back into the sister we used to know.''

She smiled, aware of how her family's information network could rival the FBI's. Within fifteen minutes after she hung up, Derek would have passed along the latest update.

"Oh, hey," he added, "I hear Galen is at Hope, too. You're in good hands."

Her blood pressure jumped twenty points. "What's that supposed to mean?" If he'd called Galen and asked him to keep an eye on her again, she'd make Derek rue the day he'd ever thought of the idea. She and Galen had reached a truce, of sorts, and she didn't need any outside interference.

"Calm down. I didn't mean anything except that he's a good man. Steady. Reliable."

She made a note to pass his description to Galen. After making himself sound like the Ultimate Bad Boy, he'd be pleased to know he'd broken free of his label, at least in Derek's eyes.

"And, anyway, you can't blame us for worrying about you," he said, sounding hurt although she knew he was only pretending. "Hope isn't even on the map."

"It is, too," she scolded gently, aware that any place with a population of less than fifty thousand didn't exist in Derek's opinion. "Everything's fine."

"OK, but I reserve the right to pay you a visit and see for myself."

"Warn me beforehand, so I can be sure I'm not on duty." With the mutual awareness simmering between herself and Galen, it was only a matter of time before it rolled to a full boil. When that happened, she didn't want to worry about her brother interrupting them.

"Will do. So what sort of night life does Hope have?"

"The ice-cream parlour is a hot spot," she replied, thinking of Galen's Wednesday evening excursion. She wasn't naïve enough to believe that a few nights on the town meant he was ready to settle down with one woman, much less her, but in all fairness, he deserved a second chance to prove it.

"A local jazz band gives concerts on Wednesdays and the American Legion baseball team plays on Thursdays. I think Friday is movie night."

"Geez, Nikki. With a harrowing schedule like that, do you have time for a shift at the hospital?"

She laughed at his wry tone. "I do, believe me."

"Where will you go after Hope?"

"I don't know yet. Don't worry. I won't be unemployed," she teased, knowing that he was asking when she'd settle down and choosing to ignore his question for now. Once she conquered her insecurities and truly believed that she was Galen's *last* rather than his *latest*— that he really was as ready for commitment and family ties as he claimed—she'd make the long-term plans her family wanted to hear.

He laughed. "I should hope not. Mom and Dad would croak if they thought those years of med school went to waste."

She chuckled. "They won't." Seeing Lynette in the doorway, chart in hand, she quickly straightened in her chair. "Gotta run. Give my love to everybody," she added, before she broke the connection.

"What do we have?" she asked her nurse.

"A lady brought her three-month-old in for a check-up. She's new in town and doesn't have a family physician, so she wanted you to check out her little one until she finds a regular doctor. I put her in the Bambi room."

The Bambi room was designed for their younger patients. The walls were tan and a forest mural, complete with a doe and her baby, covered one wall.

Nikki took the chart and went into the room. "I'm Dr Lawrence," she said, greeting the young mother who appeared to be in her late twenties.

"I'm Alice Martin," the brunette said as she shook her hand while juggling the baby in her arm. "And this is Emma."

Nikki peered at the infant who was wearing a frilly white dress with pink trim. Her long dark eyelashes lay against her cheeks and she slept contentedly as she worked her rosebud mouth as if dreaming about food.

"What a pretty dress," Nikki exclaimed, before she ran her gaze down the numbers Lynette had recorded.

"Thank you. She had her picture taken this morning and I bought this for the occasion."

"She's adorable. According to this, your daughter is right in the middle of the height and weight range for her age. If you'll give her to me, I'll check her over from top to bottom."

Nikki accepted the bundle, smiling as Emma arched her back and stretched. "Working out a few kinks, are you?" she murmured softly.

"She's quite active," Alice commented, hovering nearby. "She sleeps on her back, but I keep her on her tummy as much as possible when she's awake."

"Excellent."

"She loves music, playing in her bathwater and squeaky toys. I also read her to sleep every night. It must work because she sleeps until morning."

Nikki smiled at Alice's report. The woman clearly doted on her child. "One can't foster a bookworm too early," she said, remembering how her adoptive parents had read to her and Derek each night.

"Do you like children, Dr Lawrence?"

"Absolutely." Nikki had considered going into pediatrics, but the excitement of the ER had lured her away.

"Do you have kids?"

"I'm not married, but when I am I intend to have several."

Nikki lifted Emma's dress and listened to her chest sounds. "Has she received her three-month inoculations?"

"Last week. Before we moved."

She undid Emma's diaper. "Let's check out things down under," she crooned, just as a faint musical tune came from Alice's shoulder-bag.

Without a word, Alice dug out a cellphone and glanced at the display. "Sorry, I know it shouldn't be on. Would you excuse me?" she asked, her gaze upon her daughter lying on the table rather than on Nikki.

"Sure." Nikki continued her exam while the other woman slipped into the hall. "We aren't going anywhere, are we?"

Emma opened her eyes and blinked, then she stared at Nikki with large, deep blue eyes that would probably turn as dark as her hair.

"Hi, sweet-pea," Nikki crooned as she retaped the diaper. "Don't worry. Your mama will be back in a few minutes. She just went outside."

Emma started to fuss and Nikki immediately held her so that the infant's head rested on her shoulder. Content with that position, Emma quieted and Nikki scribbled her notes with her free hand.

Two minutes stretched to three, then four. Then five. After ten minutes, Nikki stepped into the hallway.

It was empty.

Puzzled, Nikki walked up and down the corridor, peek-

ing in every room along the way until she ended at the
reception desk.

"Have you seen Mrs Martin?" she asked Lynette.

"Not since I left her with you. Maybe she's in the restroom."

"I checked on my way here. She isn't in there."

Lynette frowned. "How odd."

Galen suddenly appeared behind her. "What's odd?"
He noticed the bundle in Nikki's arm. "Whose baby?"

"She's my patient. Emma's mother's disappeared."

He blinked. "People don't just vanish. She has to be
somewhere in the hospital."

"We've looked."

"Then look again."

Nikki, with the help of Galen, Lynette, and their fifty-
five-year-old receptionist, Jean, searched every nook and
cranny in the minor emergency clinic. When that proved
fruitless, they split up and expanded their territory to include the hospital's main lobby and the ER.

Thirty minutes and several unanswered pages for Alice
Martin later, they met again at Jean's desk.

"It's obvious what happened," Galen stated matter-of-
factly.

"What's obvious?" Nikki asked, bouncing the infant
who had started to fuss in earnest.

"Emma's been abandoned."

CHAPTER FOUR

"ABANDONED?" Nikki stared at Galen in horror. "I don't believe it."

"Deny it all you want, but Alice Martin is gone and you're holding her baby."

"You don't understand," she insisted. "I know it looks bad, but Mrs Martin doted on her daughter. She wouldn't just walk away and leave her. Why, she told me all about her likes, dislikes, and even her routine."

"Really." He didn't sound or look convinced as he raised an eyebrow. "I'd say she was passing along information so you'd know a little bit about young Emma. This woman definitely knew what she was doing."

Nikki felt sick inside. "I thought she was a typical new mother who couldn't stop talking about her baby. I didn't realize…"

"I doubt if she intended for you to know what she had planned."

"But how could she have received a phone call at the right moment?"

"She had an accomplice."

She shook her head. "The timing was too perfect. If I'd been called away or had had a number of patients waiting ahead of her, the other individual wouldn't have known that."

"Unless he was close by and could watch what was going on. It could also have been a case of blind luck."

Nikki didn't like the idea of this entire scenario being orchestrated to such great lengths. Would a woman who had bought a pretty new dress for her infant's photo leave her with a complete stranger? She didn't think so.

"Mrs Martin didn't fit the picture of a woman who'd abandon her baby. She was well dressed, spoke as if she was educated, and was concerned about Emma's care."

"You're stereotyping."

"Maybe."

"There's another option to consider. Little Miss Emma may have been kidnapped."

"Kidnapped?"

"Sure. The guilty party may be starting to feel the heat, so she decided to dump her evidence, i.e. abandon Emma where she'd be found."

The thought was horrifying, but Nikki read the papers and listened to the television news. It happened.

"I know appearances can be deceiving," she said slowly, "but I'd like to believe that Mrs Martin simply ran outside for a minute to deal with her phone call."

"There isn't any way to sugar-coat the facts, Nik. She left and didn't take her baby with her."

She frowned, and ignored his comment. "Maybe she got hit by a car or something. We should check the parking lot."

"There have been enough people in and out that some-one would have noticed if she were lying on the street," he said wryly. "If she needed medical assistance, someone would have paged me on the double."

She hated it when she couldn't argue because he was right.

He glanced at his watch. "It's been nearly an hour," he pointed out. "We'll have to notify the authorities."

"No!" Emma began to cry in earnest and Nikki soft-ened her tone. "No. Let's give Mrs Martin more time. I'm sure she has a reasonable explanation for disappearing without a trace.''

''We lock the doors in thirty minutes,'' Lynette reminded her.

Nikki turned to Galen. ''Surely we don't have to do anything for another half-hour.''

''Other than find a baby bottle?'' he asked dryly.

She smiled down at the baby, who was frowning. ''That should be first on our agenda, shouldn't it, sweet-pea?'' She glanced up at Galen. ''I'm sure I saw a diaper bag in the exam room. Let's look in there.''

Nikki hurried back to the Bambi room, conscious of Galen keeping pace. To her relief, the oversized bag rested on the floor in the corner. She hadn't noticed it before, but in light of what had happened, the bag was much larger than most and still bulged at the seams.

''Check it, will you?'' she asked, as she jostled Emma to divert her attention from her hungry tummy. ''Surely you'll find her formula.''

Galen hoisted the bag onto the table and began unzipping pouches. ''You're in luck,'' he said as he pulled a bottle out of a special insulated section designed to hold an ice pack.

Nikki grabbed it and headed for their lounge, hoping they had some means to warm the bottle. If not, a trip to the cafeteria would be in order. ''OK, sweet-pea. You'll get to eat. Just give me a minute.''

Not expert on the daily care and feeding of a baby, Nikki gratefully accepted Lynette's help. Before long, Emma was happily slurping away her dinner in Nikki's arms while Nikki brushed away the big tears clinging to her eyelashes.

''Goodness gracious,'' she crooned. ''Do you always eat

this fast? You don't want to have a tummyache when your mama comes to get you.''

"She won't be coming back.''

Nikki glanced up as Galen spoke from the doorway, his tone flat. He walked into the room, carrying a sheaf of papers and looking quite grim as he towered over her.

"Are you sure?'' Nikki asked. "How do you know?''

"Because of these.'' He waved the pages under her nose.

"Well? What are they?''

"They're documents granting temporary custody to you.''

Nikki's jaw dropped at his announcement. "Let me see,'' she demanded, certain he was wrong and needing more proof.

He handed her the top page and she quickly scanned the legal jargon, only to discover that Galen hadn't been wrong. Her name appeared as Emma's interim guardian.

"Oh…my…gosh.'' Stunned, she didn't know what else to say. The situation was too strange to be believed and, even with her name in print, she wasn't completely convinced.

She shifted her gaze to Galen. "There has to be a mistake. I can't possibly look after a baby…''

He appeared as baffled as she felt. "You're Nicole Marie Lawrence, aren't you?''

"Yes, but—''

"An Alice M. Martin has granted temporary custody of Emma A. Martin to you as of today.''

"But why would she do that? I never met her before.''

"It doesn't matter. According to this document, which is signed by an attorney and notarized, you have custody of Emma until Alice returns or for the next three months, whichever occurs first.''

Custody! For three months! ''And then what?''

''It isn't spelled out. I presume Mrs Martin will come back for her by then or she'll make other arrangements. If not, Emma will end up in foster-care.''

Foster-care. Of all words spoken, those were the two that penetrated her haze of disbelief and forced her to stop thinking about her own inadequacies for her unexpected responsibilities. If Nikki were caught in a situation where she had to choose between an impersonal Social Services bureaucracy who might or might not return her baby and a doctor who was theoretically capable of caring for an infant's needs and who most likely wouldn't fight her for custody, there wasn't any doubt which alternative she'd pick.

But this wasn't her alternative and being caught up in Alice's made this entire situation seem like a weird dream.

Another thought came to her. ''But, Galen, I'm only going to be in Hope for two months. If Alice doesn't come for her by then…''

''Then I guess you'll take Emma with you. Unless, of course, you decide not to keep her in the first place.'' He raised one eyebrow.

She shrugged helplessly. ''I don't know what to do.'' Eyeing him closely, she added, ''You seem rather calm about all this.''

''Believe me, I'm just as surprised as you are,'' he said wryly, ''even if it isn't obvious.''

He sank beside her on the lumpy sofa and shuffled the other papers. ''This lady was certainly thorough. She covered all her bases and gave you a copy of her birth certificate, medical records, and her attorney's address and phone number in case of an emergency.''

''Maybe he can explain what's going on.''

''Maybe.'' He pulled out a thick, sealed manila envelope. "And maybe this will hold all the answers to your questions."

She eyed her name written on the front in feminine script. Slowly, she accepted the envelope.

"I'll take her so you can read your letter." He held out his arms and began handling little Emma like a pro as he patted her back until she let loose a burp that was bigger than she was.

While Galen murmured to the baby, Nikki carefully unsealed the glued flap and drew out a sheet of rose-patterned stationery.

> *Dear Dr Lawrence,*
>
> *By now, you've realized what a huge duty I've thrust upon you. I apologize for dragging you into my desperate situation and sharing so few facts, but know that I would never have left Emma with anyone if my circumstances weren't dire. After watching you this past week…*

Nikki stopped reading. Mrs Martin had *watched* her? How? When? She continued.

> *After watching you this past week and deciding what to do, I realized that you are my only hope and the best answer for Emma's continued well-being and safety. I wish I could give you more details, but I can't yet. I will explain everything when I see you again.*

I certainly hope so, Nikki thought.

> *My only stipulation is that you must swear to complete secrecy about Emma's identity and how she arrived in your care. If you cannot do so for whatever*

reasons, please speak with my attorney, Howard Finch, immediately. I can't emphasize the importance of keeping this information and these circumstances confidential.

Look after the treasure I've given you, Nikki.

It gave Nikki an eerie feeling to read her nickname. While it wasn't any secret that she answered to ''Nikki'', only Galen knew her well enough to use it.

Assure her every day of my love and tell her that I will see her soon.

Please contact my lawyer if, for any reason, there is an emergency. Otherwise I'll see you in three months, if not before.

Rest assured that I will return for the love of my life unless it is physically impossible. If that unfortunate situation should occur, Mr Finch will pass along my final instructions.

Sincerely,
Alice M. Martin
P.S. Use the money for whatever Emma needs while in your care.

Nikki peeked in the large envelope and saw a smaller one lying in the bottom. She left it for now and focused instead on the letterhead of Finch, Finch, and Brown, attorneys-at-law. His letter was a repeat of Alice's and included both his office and unlisted private phone numbers.

She stared at the pages, hardly able to believe their contents, but she had no choice. Alice's plan, such as it was, was loosely outlined, which, along with the lawyer's letter, proved that this hadn't been a spur-of-the-moment decision. The question was, could she take on this responsibility?

"Well?" Galen demanded, impatient for Nikki's response and easily able to see how stunned she was by these events.

"Alice assures me that she loves her daughter and will return for her."

"Did she say why she left her?"

Nikki shook her head. "Do you want me to take her now?"

"Nah," he said. Emma was sleeping in the crook of his arm, so he didn't want to jostle her awake. Truthfully, he rather enjoyed holding a baby that wasn't screaming blue murder because it was in pain or scared of the strange man poking and prodding it. "What *did* she say?"

"Just that she had to do this. Something about Emma's safety. Read it for yourself."

Galen took the page and scanned the handwriting. "Do you think she's telling the truth, or just playing on your sympathies?"

"Then you don't think I should get involved?"

"Part of me wants to warn you that you could be setting yourself up for something ugly."

"In other words, if Mrs Martin is hiding from the law…"

"Precisely. On the other hand…" he gazed at the infant snuggled against his chest, one tiny hand clutching his lab coat in a tight-fisted grip "…the situation could be just as she's described. That she's desperate and you were part of her temporary solution."

He hesitated. "What are you going to do?"

"I don't know. I'm completely overwhelmed."

"You can always call the attorney and decline."

Her gaze met his. "Do you think I should?"

Galen ran his free hand through his hair. "I'm tempted to say yes, but I suspect you won't agree."

"You're right. I can't. Emma isn't a package we can just pass around, waiting for someone to accept it."

He drew a bracing breath, hoping that Nikki understood what she was getting herself into. "Are you sure? How are you going to take care of her?"

"The same way every other mother does."

"You don't have any paraphernalia," he pointed out. "Babies require a lot of equipment."

"That's not a problem. Alice mentioned that she'd enclosed money." She dug out the smaller envelope and gasped as she opened it. "Ohmigosh."

"What?"

"There's five thousand dollars in here."

He whistled softly. "You definitely need to talk to this lady's attorney. For your protection, we also should take these papers to an attorney friend of mine for his opinion."

"You don't think they're legal?"

"I don't know, but are you willing to risk it if they aren't? According to this…" he held up the letter "…Finch's firm is in Oklahoma City, which is a long cry from Hope. For all we know, he could have gotten his law degree off the Internet and is operating out of his basement."

"Can people do that?" she asked, sounding curious. "Get law degrees off the Internet?"

"I don't know, but for the right price I'm sure you can get any sort of degree you want. The point is, we don't know anything about this guy and this is too important to make any assumptions."

"Don't worry. I'm convinced."

"But we've gotten off the subject of how you intend to take care of her. You can't bring her to work with you."

"I'll make day-care arrangements."

"Overnight? I hate to disappoint you, but from the complaints I've heard from the younger ER staff, it can take weeks to find someone who has an opening, especially for an infant."

"I didn't say it would be easy, Galen."

He tried again. "What about sleepless nights and all that? Caring for her alone means you'll be the only one who will get up in the middle of the night for her."

"I've lost sleep before," she countered. "And Alice assured me that Emma rarely wakes up at night."

He ached to know how this would interfere with his own plans for Nikki, but instantly decided that this could be a blessing in disguise. Nikki would need help and he intended to supply it.

"As long as you're going into this with your eyes wide open…" he said.

"I am, provided the legal issues check out."

He rose. "Then, if you'll take her, I'll try and catch Matt at his office." He handed over the baby, noticing how natural Nikki looked with an infant in her arms. The idea of giving Nikki his baby made his body respond to the point he was grateful to be wearing a scrub suit and lab coat. If he didn't break through her insecurities soon, he was going to go crazy with frustration. Patience might be a virtue, but it was one that he didn't have where Nikki was concerned.

A phone call and a few minutes later, he reported, "I'm supposed to run over to Matt's office now. He's leaving in an hour for his son's ball game, but I can't leave the ER."

"I'll cover for you," she offered. "Maybe Lynette will stay until you come back, just in case I get busy and can't watch Emma."

Lynette appeared in the doorway with Jean right behind her. "Did I hear my name mentioned?"

"Galen is going to check on a few things for me so I'm going to cover the ER," Nikki said. "Can you hang around to look after Emma?"

"Sure. Just let me call home and tell my kids I'll be late."

"They won't mind?"

"Not if I promise to bring home fast food."

Nikki smiled. "Then it's my treat."

"One more thing," Galen cautioned the trio. "It's important for no one to know how Emma came to be here."

"I don't understand," Lynette said, clearly puzzled.

Nikki summarized the story. "For now I've been granted temporary custody, so we'll have to think of a plausible cover story."

Jean, a widow who devoured mystery fiction and arranged her life according to the air times of police drama and crime scene investigation television shows, immediately perked up. "This is fantastic. Just like on TV. Maybe Mrs Martin is on the lam. Or she's trying to run away from an abusive husband. Or—"

"No one is supposed to know anything about Emma," Galen warned her, hoping the woman would tamp down her enthusiasm. "As for speculating, don't. I'm sure there's a simple explanation, so let's not blow it out of proportion. People will notice if we act like we're hiding something."

"We are," Lynette pointed out, "but I won't say a word."

"Don't worry about me either. My lips are sealed." Jean clamped her mouth shut, then made a turning motion to simulate a key being turned.

"Then it's settled." Galen used his physician's authoritative voice that few dared to argue with. "We'll all go about our business. This weekend we'll think of a good cover story for why Nikki is looking after Emma and let you know on Monday."

Jean and Lynette nodded before they left to lock up the office.

Galen turned to Nikki. "I'll hurry back."

She smiled at him. "We'll be waiting."

"What did you find out?" Nikki asked Galen an hour and a half later when he arrived at her apartment. His visit to Matt's office had lasted longer than expected because Matt had tried to learn more about Mr Finch through his network of legal friends. Impatient to go home, Nikki had left immediately after she'd handed the ER reins over to Galen's evening shift colleague, Ivan Tesler.

"Apparently Howard Finch is a well-respected member of the Oklahoma City legal community," Galen said as he glanced around her living room. "You've been busy."

Nikki had unpacked the bag Alice had supplied and now its contents covered her sofa and coffee-table. There were clothes of all kinds, several soft, squishy, and squeaky toys, three cardboard books, which were obviously Emma's bedtime reading material, the requisite baby shampoo, soap, ointments, cleansing wipes and powder, a supply of bottles, and several containers of formula.

"I only found a couple of diapers," she told him. "We'll definitely have to run to the store tonight because three won't tide us over until morning."

"OK." He looked around. "Speaking of the one who needs that particular item, where's Emma?"

"In bed." She grinned. "Actually, she's in my suit-case."

"Your suitcase?"

"It was the best I could do on short notice," she said, leading the way into her bedroom where she'd placed her largest, soft-sided piece of luggage on the floor and lined it with towels and a sheet.

"I'll buy a crib tomorrow, but she can't mind it too much," she added in a whisper, "because she's still sleeping."

"You'd better wake her up or she won't sleep tonight," he warned.

"I will. In a few minutes." She shooed him from the room, leaving the door ajar so she could hear the baby if she cried. "First, I want to hear the rest of the story."

"Matt says the papers are in order. Emma is yours. Temporarily. Unless…" His voice faded.

Wariness filled her soul. "Unless what?"

"Unless you call Finch and say you can't handle this."

"It's too late."

His eyes narrowed and she felt his scrutiny. "Too late?"

"I've already called him."

"And?" he demanded.

"And after listening to him, I decided to keep Emma, just as her mother intended." Actually, she'd come to her decision *before* she'd spoken to Mr Finch, and their conversation had simply cemented the deal. Her earlier comment about Emma being passed around like an unwanted package had hit closer to the mark than Galen had realized. She, too, had been moved from one foster-home to another before she'd finally found a permanent adoptive home with the Lawrence family. While Emma was too young to remember this time in her life, Nikki wasn't convinced that she wouldn't subconsciously pick up the same feelings of rejection that Nikki had suffered. For that reason, barring any illegal activity, she would do whatever was necessary to keep Emma until her mother returned. No matter what.

A deep wrinkle of apparent frustration appeared on his forehead. "I thought you were going to wait until I talked to Matt."

"I was," she agreed, eager to smooth his ruffled feathers. "I only wanted to ask him a few questions to help me make up my mind. He started telling me not to worry, that Alice wanted the very best for her child and that he was sorry about being unable to explain the exact circumstances because of client confidentiality, but that he wouldn't have been a party to this if he'd had reservations. He sounded so nice and was so convincing—"

"Of course he was," Galen retorted. "He's a lawyer. He's supposed to be convincing."

"I didn't call with the purpose of agreeing to anything. If you'd been here, you would have heard my side of the conversation for yourself."

"That's my point. I *wasn't*, and I should have been!"

"Why?" she asked calmly. "Give me a little credit for knowing my own mind, Galen. And you shouldn't be angry. You found out the same thing I did."

"But what if I hadn't?" He ran his hands through his hair. "No wonder your brothers are always worried about you leaping before you look."

"Galen," she warned, stiffening her spine to add an extra inch to her height, "you know yourself that sometimes you just have to go with your instincts. In this case, I chose to go with mine. I'm sorry if that has offended you..."

"I'm not offended, Nik," he said as he wrapped his arms around her. "Only afraid you'll get into something way over your head."

"I won't."

"You don't know that."

"Sure I do." She grinned at him. "Between my intuition and your suspicious nature, we'll be fine."

One eyebrow raised. "Suspicious nature?"

"I mean it in the nicest possible way," she teased.

"I'll bet."

"Seriously, though, we need to plan our story. But first…" she cocked her head to listen to the squeaks of unhappiness drifting in from the bedroom "…we're being paged."

Nikki took care of Emma's wet bottom while Galen warmed her formula. As soon as Emma was occupied with her bottle, Galen sat beside Nikki on the sofa.

"Do you have any ideas on how to plausibly explain why you're minding a baby?" he asked.

"I thought about saying she's my niece. No one would think twice if they thought I was taking care of my brother's baby."

"For three months?"

"They're out of the country."

"What for?"

"An archeological dig in Egypt."

"Isn't that rather clichéd? And what if someone asks about their project?"

Nikki shrugged. "Then I say that it has something to do with old pots and other than that I'm clueless."

"What if someone discovers that your brothers don't have children? Then there's the question of why *you're* taking care of the baby rather than your parents. If word gets back to them that you have an infant in your apartment who's supposedly a relative, are you prepared for them to descend and ask questions?"

"Ohmigosh. That's right. Derek said he was coming to visit and since I'd told him that he could, the rest will, too."

He nodded matter-of-factly. "That also sinks the idea of Emma being your cousin's baby."

"You're right."

"What about a friend?"

She thought for a moment. "They know most of my friends and if I'm a close enough friend to do this, they'll wonder why I've never mentioned Emma's mother."

"You're running out of legitimate options," he reminded her. "If she's not a relative, then she has to be a friend's baby. Otherwise you can't justify having her."

"OK. Emma will be my friend Alice Martin's baby. They've never met her because…" She thought quickly. "She moved to away right after college and we lost touch until recently."

"And why did she give her to you?"

Nikki thought fast. "Because she's in the Navy and being deployed on a training mission."

"For three months?"

"So my timing's off to be completely accurate, but do you have a better excuse?"

"No. I suppose if Alice returns early and if your brothers never come for a visit, it won't matter what our story is."

"Exactly." She raised Emma to her shoulder and patted her until the required burp resounded.

"I think we're ready to go shopping," she told Galen.

"We'll take my car," he said, rising. "It's bigger than yours."

Nikki stared at him in surprise. "Do you really want to tag along?"

"Of course," he said a trifle impatiently. "If you think I'm letting you struggle through these next few months on your own, you're deluding yourself."

"Is this another case of you deciding what's best for me?" she asked. "Of saving me from myself?"

"No," he said slowly. "I'm simply saying that, sink or swim, we're in this together."

CHAPTER FIVE

"WE SHOULD probably find a bed for Emma while we're here," Galen said as he secured the infant carrier on the shopping cart Nikki had freed from the cart corral inside the discount store.

"I'd rather look for a used crib in the classifieds," she said.

"What if you don't find one?" he asked pragmatically. "Do you want to explain to her mother that you allowed Emma to sleep in a suitcase for two months?"

"No," she answered slowly. "But they're so expensive…"

"Alice left money with you so you can buy what Emma needs. Expensive or not, the kid needs a bed. If you're worried, I'll chip in—"

"I'm not arguing about buying a bed, but we don't have to rush into purchasing something that neither of us will use after she leaves."

Nikki might not want to think past the next few months, but he did. He hoped that he and Nikki would put that same crib to use within the next year or two. He wasn't getting any younger and he wanted to have kids of his own while he still had enough energy to run after them.

"OK," he conceded, "but can we at least *look*?" He had a feeling that once she saw their selection and he expounded on the benefits of sleeping on a mattress, she'd change her mind.

His own thought pulled him up short. *The benefits of sleeping on a mattress.* The image that popped into his

79

head didn't include little Emma, only her guardian, and he forced it away for a later time.

"Looking won't hurt," she admitted. "But we're not buying anything unless it's on sale."

"You're the boss." He'd humor her for now because he suspected that convincing her to browse meant the battle was half-won.

"Why are you so concerned about a bed for her?" she asked as she pushed the cart toward the infant department. "Emma doesn't care where she sleeps."

"No, but I do. A bona fide crib is much safer, too. It isn't as if you were only keeping her for a night or two. You're her mother for three months."

"Geez. I am, aren't I?"

Nikki sounded awed and a little scared of her responsibility. "Yeah, you are."

She stopped in her tracks. "What if I can't do this? What if I make a mistake? If anything happens…"

A lesser man might have told her to get out while she was still ahead, to call the lawyer again and tell him that she'd changed her mind, but Galen suspected she was simply experiencing a case of new-mom jitters. Being gallant, he intended to help dispel her fears.

Idly, he realized he'd done this before…and with horrible consequences. This time he'd simply have to handle it right. He didn't have any room for error.

"You'll be fine," he told her. "You're a doctor. You can handle anything that comes your way. And I'll be here to help. All you have to do is say the word."

He wanted her to say "I do", but that was two words and the appropriate answer to an entirely different question. The key to success lay in the timing, and at the moment the timing was off by a country mile.

"Remember what I told you before we left your apartment. We're in this together. I meant it."

Her mouth curved into a tremulous smile. "You're right. For a minute, I'd forgotten."

"Don't." He drew her close to his side in a one-armed hug of encouragement. Little did she know that he simply couldn't keep his hands off her, but if he couldn't touch her the way he wanted—even though it was killing him— he'd settle for this platonic stuff. For now.

"Are you ever going to explain why you agreed to take on Emma's care in the first place?" he asked.

"Later," she said, as they entered the section of the store filled with everything a baby could possibly need, and then some. "We have shopping to do."

He gazed at the aisles for assorted baby supplies and the rows of clothing racks. He hadn't felt this overwhelmed since his first day of medical school. "I'm glad you didn't send me by myself."

"Why?"

He motioned toward the shelves. "Too many choices. A man could spend hours just trying to figure out which disposable diaper to buy."

She giggled. "You've seen babies of all sizes in the ER. They don't show up with the same one-size-fits-all diaper."

"I never really noticed or thought about it," he admitted. "As long as the darn thing was doing its job, I didn't pay attention to if it was pink or blue, had ruffles or elastic on the legs." He picked up a package. "Or if the spots changed color when wet."

"You need to pay attention to those details now," she said. "If we're in this together, as you said, then the chances are good you'll have to make an emergency diaper run or two. So be prepared."

"Yes, ma'am," he said dutifully, memorizing the appearance of the package Nikki placed in the cart. "Is forty-eight enough?"

"Now that you mention it…" She tossed another package in the cart. "Better not take any chances. I don't want to come back in few days."

He mentally rang up the cost. No wonder people were thrilled when their kids were potty-trained.

"While I'm getting a few other things for her," she added, "can you grab the formula?"

"What kind?" He may not have been in this part of the store before, but he'd talked to drug reps during his stint in pediatrics and knew there were scores of brands with all sorts of additional supplement combinations.

Nikki pulled a label out of her purse. "Get enough to last the week."

"How often and how much does she eat?"

"Buy a case."

"A case? Twenty-four cans? She surely won't gobble down that much in a week."

"All right. That number does seem excessive. Make that a half a case."

"Half a case," he dutifully repeated, still thinking it was far too many—but what did he know about the daily care and feeding of a baby? He might know the theory, but theory didn't always stand up to actual experience.

He reached out to tickle Emma's chin. "If you keep this up," he teased her as she chortled with delight, "we'll have to rename you Piglet."

"If the only food going into your mouth was milk, you'd eat a lot, too."

"I suppose, but, honestly, you want *twelve* cans?"

She shrugged. "Do you want to come back in a few

days? Or would you rather I woke you at midnight and sent you out to buy her formula then?''

''OK. I get the picture. Half a case, coming right up.''

He strolled down the appropriate aisle with label in hand and Nikki on his mind. He wouldn't care if she woke him at any time, day or night, as long as she was nestled beside him when it happened—snuggled against him with an arm and a leg draped over his and nothing but skin between them.

An ache that had become increasingly familiar ever since Nikki had come to town began to build. He shouldn't be torturing himself like this, he mentally reprimanded himself. Until he convinced Nikki that he had changed his ways, he didn't have a snowball's chance in hell of turning his imaginings into reality.

''Why, hel-lo, Galen,'' came a flirtatious voice. ''Whatever are you doing here?''

He turned unseeing eyes away from the rows of stacked cans to find Annabelle Sanders, a blonde he'd taken out a few times several months ago, standing next to him.

Damn!

''Just shopping,'' he answered politely, hoping to send her on her way before Nikki returned.

''And what are you doing these days?'' she asked coyly. ''I haven't seen you around.''

''Just working. You know the story…too many sick people and not enough docs to go around.''

''Don't you know that all work and no play isn't good for you?''

She slowly straightened his collar as if it were her right to do so. Six months ago he wouldn't have minded. Now he did. The only woman's touch he wanted to feel was Nikki's.

''I've heard that.'' He stepped out of range and grabbed

the first can he saw off the shelf. Realizing it was the wrong one, he replaced it.

"If you ever have any free time, give me a call."

"With things as they are," he said, being purposely vague, "I probably won't."

"Too bad." Suddenly her eyes narrowed, as if she was speculating on why he happened to be in this particular part of the store in the first place. "Formula, Galen?"

"I'm helping a friend."

"Ah." She sounded satisfied with his answer. "You do look rather lost. Can I help?"

He finally noticed what he hadn't before. Annabelle wore a red store smock and name tag, so this was obviously her assigned area. From the way she moved in close to him, she also intended to offer more personal merchandise than what her employer stocked.

Great. Just what he needed. First Trina, the waitress at the restaurant, and now Annabelle. If Nikki saw her…

"Is this your department?" He mentally crossed his fingers, hoping it was not.

"Oh, no. I cover the intimate apparel." She winked. "But when I walked by and saw you, I just had to stop and say hello."

How lucky could a man get? he thought glumly. Fortunately, he spied the brand he needed and began scooping cans into his arms.

"Thanks for the offer, but I found what I need."

"You don't have a cart. Let me help you," she said, taking a can out of his hand and tucking it in the crook of her arm.

Before Galen could decline, he heard Nikki's voice. "Oh, good. You found her formula."

He turned, wishing that his past hadn't collided with his future twice in the same evening.

"I did." He hastily loaded his cans in the cart, tucking them around the other items Nikki had already stacked inside. "Do we have everything now?"

"I think so," she said calmly. "But won't you introduce me to your friend?"

Damn! "Nikki Lawrence, Annabelle Sanders. Annabelle, Nikki. Now, are we ready?"

Nikki smiled at Annabelle, apparently not in as big a hurry to leave as he was. "I'm pleased to meet you."

Galen mentally groaned in spite of the smile he'd pasted on his face.

"Yeah. Same here," the other woman responded, although curiosity was clearly eating at her. "I'd better get back to my department before I'm missed. See you around, Galen. Take care of yourself."

"I will." If he ever did see Annabelle again, it would be by accident rather than by choice.

Nikki waggled her fingers in a goodbye wave, then headed toward the furniture display. "Isn't it nice that we're running into so many of your friends?"

Certain he would step into quicksand if he wasn't careful, he changed the subject. "What sort of crib are you looking for?"

"I'm not sure." She pushed the cart toward the closest one. "What do you think of this type?"

Pleased that he'd diverted her attention, he relaxed and stood next to a white crib. "It's OK. Do you want it wood-stained or painted?"

"I prefer the wood look. How long have you known Annabelle?"

"Not long. What about this one?" He stood in front of another baby bed.

She eyed it, then shook her head. "Nice, but too expensive. We don't need one that converts to a day bed or has drawers underneath. A basic bed will do. Do you know Annabelle as an acquaintance, or was she more than that?''

"We went out a few times to dinner and a movie. This metal crib is different. Unusual."

She shook her head. "Too institutional-looking, even with the fancy curliques. After seeing her in action, I think she'd like to go out again."

Galen was getting tired of holding two conversations at once.

"Yeah, but it isn't going to happen. What do you think of this sleigh bed?" He busied himself by examining it closely.

"It's nice, but not what I had in mind. Is there any woman in town you *haven't* dated?"

"You," he answered promptly.

A smile tugged on her mouth. "What do you call what we're doing tonight?"

"Maybe I'm old-fashioned, but shopping for diapers and dining with a baby doesn't constitute a date."

"It could count."

"But it won't." On this he was firm. "When we go to dinner without Miss Piglet, just you and me, we'll call it a date." He moved to the last crib on display—a model that met all of her requirements from the stain color to being on a close-out sale. "What do you think about this one?"

"It has potential," she said, running her hand along the straight headboard. "Other than me, *is* there anyone in Hope who hasn't had the privilege of an evening with the most eligible Dr Galen Stafford?"

"Yes, there are, but don't ask for a list because I don't know their names. Neither do I want to know them. Now, can we, *please*, focus on the baby bed and not my past love life?" He emphasized *past* for her benefit.

Her gentle smile was as soothing as the touch of her hand on his arm. "You're right. We're here for a bed, nothing else. I'm sorry for teasing you, Galen, but I couldn't resist it."

She'd been *teasing*? "Then you don't mind about the others?" he asked cautiously.

"I didn't say that I didn't mind," she answered slowly. "However, I'm mature enough to accept that you haven't lived like a monk. The important thing is what happens from now on."

He'd expected her dander to rise, and had received an unexpected dose of mercy. Relieved, he hauled her beside him for a quick but semi-satisfying hug. "I couldn't have said it better."

Emma's soft gurgles slowly became higher-pitched. "I think she's feeling neglected," Nikki said as Galen reluctantly released her.

"I know the feeling," he murmured.

Nikki lifted the baby out of her infant carrier and held her to her shoulder. "We're hurrying, sweet-pea," she crooned. "As soon as we pay for your new bed, we're going home."

Home. He liked the sound of that.

On Monday morning, Nikki raced into the MEC, feeling as if she was already behind before her day had started. "I'm sorry I'm late," she apologized to Jean and Lynette. "After being a model baby all weekend, Emma decided not to co-operate this morning."

Lynette grinned. "Babies sense when to throw a kink in the works, don't they? My kids were the same way. When we didn't have a time schedule to follow, they were great. When we did, I could count on having a major incident. So what did she do?"

"You don't want to know," Nikki said darkly. "Suffice it to say that it required another bath."

Jean wrinkled her nose. "Ooh. One of *those*."

"Yeah. Just when we were getting ready to walk out of the door, too." She tossed her purse in a file cabinet behind Jean for safekeeping. "So, who's first?"

"We are," Jean answered. "You don't get to see any patients until we know the story."

"The *full* story," Lynette added. "No one's here, anyway, so don't leave out any details."

"OK, here goes." Nikki drew a deep breath. "Emma is the daughter of a friend of mine who is in the military and was sent on a training mission. She brought Emma by on Friday and will be back for her in a few months."

Jean looked thoughtful. "That sounds credible."

"Galen and I thought so, too."

"But what about taking care of her in the meantime?" Lynette asked. "I assume you found a sitter?"

"I took her to the hospital day care this morning."

"I thought they were full."

"I'd heard that, too, but Galen knows Susan O'Conner, the director. He called her and she agreed to watch Emma since it would only be short term."

Once Nikki had learned that Susan was a divorcee, she suspected that Susan had been more than willing to do a favor—*any* favor—for Galen. For all Nikki knew, the two of them had gone out at some point, but she didn't press him for details like she had with Trina and Annabelle. Just because she was trying to be mature in recognizing and accepting his past for what it was, it didn't mean she wanted to face it every time she turned round. What she didn't know wouldn't hurt her.

On the other hand, she didn't want to hound him like a shrew about every woman he knew either. If this leopard sincerely had changed his spots, then she had to work on her own issues of trust and meet him halfway.

"That'll be handy," Lynette remarked. "You can run over to the child-care center for a quick cuddle whenever you have a few minutes."

"I thought so, too," Nikki confessed. "Although Galen will probably be over there as much as I will."

Jean smiled. "He's quite taken with the baby?"

"He practically spent the entire weekend at my place."

"It's a good thing he is," Jean stated in no uncertain terms. "I've been thinking about what you told us on Friday—about how her safety depended upon secrecy. It's not a bad idea for you to have someone else around in case someone tries anything funny. Why, we could be dealing with a drug lord, terrorists, or the Mob! I read this marvelous book this weekend where—"

"Let's not let our imaginations run away with us," Nikki said dryly. "As long as we stick to our story, no one will be the wiser. Understood?"

"Loud and clear," Jean said with a sniff. "I couldn't live with myself if I said anything that might cause harm to that poor baby."

"I know." Sensing that she needed to soothe Jean's ruffled feathers, Nikki patted her arm. "I'm counting on you to stay alert for any strangers asking questions about us."

"I'll let you know right away," Jean promised, her good humor now restored by the prospect of her new mission.

"If Dr Stafford spent all weekend with you," Lynette said, "what did the three of you do? Or is that confidential information?" She winked.

"Only if you consider putting Emma's new crib together and helping me move furniture as being confidential. On Sunday he brought a stroller over, insisting that she needed to look around her neighborhood. I swear we walked for miles.''

''He *is* keeping a close eye on you two.'' Jean's gaze turned speculative.

''He's only there to help me take care of Emma,'' Nikki said defensively, although her face warmed several degrees as she remembered how he'd stopped by her apartment every night last week, long before Emma had dropped into the picture. Yet the whole scenario was still too new and too fraught with difficulties in spite of his declared intent for her to imply that a romance was in the air.

''If you say so.''

''He spends a lot of time with the baby, feeding her, playing with her…''

''Changing her diapers?'' Lynette raised an eyebrow.

Nikki grinned. ''He's taken his turn.''

Lynette clapped a hand over her chest. ''Be still, my heart. My husband never changed a single one and we had three children.''

''I'm sorry to hear it.''

''Yeah, well, if he thinks he'll keep his unblemished track record after the grandkids come, he can think again.''

''It is rather sweet of Dr Stafford,'' Jean said. ''Who would have thought a baby would have turned him from a swinging single to a doting daddy?''

''Ladies, ladies.'' Nikki's face warmed another ten degrees. ''Didn't we just have a talk about runaway imaginations?''

Jean laughed. ''Yeah, and I'd like to keep mine. Life is too boring otherwise.'' She rose to unlock the patient entrance. ''You two had better get busy because my arthritis is acting up and you know what that means.''

''It's going to rain?'' Nikki answered helpfully.

''We're going to be swamped,'' Lynette explained. As

Nikki looked at her with skepticism, she shrugged. "I know, I know. As weird as it sounds, I didn't believe it either, but I'm telling you, she's right. You'll see."

Nikki did, indeed, see. Patients streamed through the door all morning until she wondered how the waiting area could hold that many. She'd just watch Lynette help a twelve-year-old girl hobble into an exam room with a bloody bandage on her foot when she heard a commotion near Jean's desk.

"Why can't I be seen now?" the man, wearing an expensive-looking tailored suit, demanded. "I have to be in court in a couple of hours."

"I'm sorry, but there are people ahead of you. People who are seriously injured," Jean tried to explain.

"Then they should be in the ER," he snapped. "It was my understanding that this area is for *minor* emergencies."

Nikki held onto her temper with difficulty. He might be a lawyer, or higher in the judicial chain, and carry enough clout to send people jumping however high with a single grunt, but he was in her domain, where *her* word was law, not his.

She interrupted. "May I help you?"

"I certainly hope so," the fellow snapped. "I'd like to see the doctor right away."

"And what's your emergency?"

"I have a mole that I want removed."

"I see." Nikki pretended to consider. "And how is your situation more critical than the young lady whose foot is bleeding or the young man with abdominal pain and a fever?"

"I'm due in court—" he began.

"And these people have places to go, too," she said sweetly. "Now, if you'll have a seat, I'll be with you shortly. Otherwise we can stand here and you can try to convince me to move you to the front of the line but, rest assured, sir, that you'll only delay your treatment and everyone else's.''

He opened his mouth to argue, then snapped it closed as if he'd realized that quarreling was futile. ''Fine,'' he said shortly as he returned to his seat, folding his arms across his chest and glaring at everyone in general and Nikki in particular.

Nikki cast a raised eyebrow at Jean, then hurried to deal with the twelve-year-old girl, who'd stepped on a nail.

''Grandpa told me not to go out to the barn unless I had my heavy shoes on,'' Lucy said tearfully, ''but I just wanted to peek at the kittens.''

Nikki unwrapped her foot and saw the puncture wound in Lucy's heel. ''Was the nail rusty?''

Lucy's grandfather answered. ''It didn't look like it when I pulled the board off her foot, but I didn't want to take any chances so I brought her here.''

''Rust or not, if it was in the barn, there are other nasty germs to worry about,'' Nikki said as she irrigated the wound. ''Did you see the kittens before you had your accident?''

Lucy nodded, wiping her eyes. ''They're really cute. Grandpa says I can take one home with me if Mom will let me. I want the black one with the white tips on her ears.''

''Lucy spends a week with us every summer,'' her grandfather said. ''This is the first time she's ever gotten hurt. I should have checked for old boards lying around before she came.''

''Well,'' Nikki said as she taped gauze over the wound, ''it's not that bad and Lucy is a young lady who simply wasn't as cautious as she knows how to be.''

Lucy nodded. ''I've never gotten hurt before.''

"Accidents do happen," Nikki said to the grandfather. "I'll give her some antibiotics to take as a precaution. Do you know if she's had a recent tetanus vaccination?"

"I don't know," he admitted.

"We'll give her one, to be on the safe side. If she hasn't had a booster since she was a baby, she's due for her TD injection anyway." Lucy was at the age when schools required students to receive a current tetanus and diptheria immunization.

"Thank you, Doctor," the older man said gratefully.

She stripped off her gloves and patted Lucy on the shoulder. "You won't be able to put your full weight on your heel for a few days, so take it easy."

"I will."

"And wear sturdy shoes when you visit the barn." She smiled.

Lucy nodded. "I learned my lesson."

Nikki's next patient was a twenty-year-old who complained of nausea and diffuse abdominal pain with rebound tenderness.

"I'm afraid you have a classic case of appendicitis," she told the lanky, bearded Arthur Richmond after her examination.

He groaned. "Aw, man, I can't have appendicitis. I have a comedy gig next week."

"Not any more," she told him. "I'm going to order some lab work just to be sure, but while we're waiting for the CBC results we'll arrange for a surgical consult."

"Surgery." He moaned once again. "Aw, I don't want to lay in the hospital for a week and have stitches. How can I perform with my gut held together by a thread?"

"Staples," she corrected. "But you probably won't have those either. I know of cases where the surgeon went through the belly button. Without complications, you're out of the hospital in a couple of days, but it will still take time for your insides to heal.''

''Aw, man. This was a good paying job, too.''

''I'm sorry but sometimes things like this happen.'' She patted his shoulder. ''Cheer up. You're healthy and we probably caught the problem before your appendix did something nasty like rupture. Then you'd be talking weeks of recuperation time.''

''Yeah, I guess.''

She smiled at his glum tone. ''Someone will be right in to draw a blood sample.''

Leaving him, she went to the next room where she found Mr Demandingly Obnoxious. According to the chart Lynette had started, his name was William H. Pettigrew, the Third.

''Thanks for being so patient, Mr Pettigrew,'' she said calmly. ''What's this about a mole?''

''On my back,'' he said as he shrugged off his shirt, revealing a well-tanned, muscular physique. ''I play tennis three mornings a week with a friend of mine and he's been hounding me to come in for an expert opinion. I've been rather busy—a big court case among other things—and I ignored it, but my friend positively insisted I do something *today*.'' He paused. ''What do you think?''

Nikki studied the offending mole in the middle of his back. At first glance, she knew his friend had cause for concern. For several reasons, she already assumed it was a melanoma. First, it was asymmetrical. Second, it had an irregular border. Third, the color was a mixture of red, brown, and black. And, fourth, its diameter was far greater than a quarter of an inch—more specifically, she guessed it to be a full inch across.

''Can you remove it right now?'' he asked.

''No,'' she said bluntly. ''I'm not a dermatologist.''

"I've had general practitioners remove moles before," he said. "Why can't you?"

"Because I suspect it's a melanoma and not a simply mole," she told him.

"Melanoma? As in skin cancer?"

"Yes."

"Then it *is* an emergency and you're required to administer appropriate medical care."

She ignored his implied threat. "You should also know that, depending on what stage it is, I could make matters worse by causing the tumor to shed cells that will spread beyond this spot." She paused. "This really is quite large. How long have you had it?"

"A year or so." His arrogance faded and worry took its place. "Am I going to die?"

"This is extremely serious," she said. "You need to take care of this right away."

"I'm trying," he burst out. "That's why I'm here."

"With a specialist who concentrates on melanomas."

He fell silent, then heaved a frustrated sigh. "OK. Where do I go and who do I see next?"

"I'll make a few phone calls while you get dressed. As soon as I've arranged an appointment, I'll be back."

She found Lynette and, after calling the name the nurse had recommended, she returned to Pettigrew's room. "Dr Everly is a dermatologist who comes here twice a week for consults. Tomorrow is one of his days and he's agreed to see you at three p.m. If that time doesn't work, you'll need to drive to his office in Oklahoma City on the day after."

He frowned. "Tomorrow isn't an optimal day. I can't wait until the next time he sees patients in Hope?"

"Time is of the essence," she told him. "The cancer

won't stop spreading because you're too busy to work treatment into your schedule.''

He exhaled. ''OK. Three o'clock tomorrow.''

''Good.'' She wrote out an order for a CBC, liver function studies, and a chest X-ray. ''Before you leave the hospital, I want you to go to the lab for blood tests and stop in at Radiology for an X-ray.''

He took the piece of paper. ''Can't these things wait until tomorrow? I need to talk to my client before—''

''I don't think you understand the gravity of your situation,'' she said firmly. ''Dr Everly will need these results so he can evaluate your condition properly. Your appointment will go much more smoothly and prevent further delays if these tests are completed now. Otherwise you risk not seeing another client. Ever.''

''Fine,'' he snapped. ''I'll go right now.''

She ushered him into the hallway, relieved that he'd agreed to take care of his problem. He might not realize it yet, but his friend's persistence just might have saved his life.

With Pettigrew off her mind, she suddenly noticed an odd, acrid smell hanging in the air. She followed her nose down the short hallway leading toward Galen's ER and caught a glimpse of a door closing at the end—a family quiet room, if she remembered correctly. Deciding that some die-hard smoker couldn't wait until he got outside to light up, she turned back.

A series of sudden loud pops sent her ducking for cover. Half turning to identify the source, she saw a flash of sparks out of the corner of her eye seconds before white smoke billowed toward her.

Fire!

CHAPTER SIX

NIKKI didn't waste time as something hot whizzed past her cheek. Mentally she ran through the catchy phrase she'd learned at her teaching facility. RACE—Rescue, Alarm, Contain, Evacuate. With no one in immediate danger except herself, and it being far bigger than she could contain on her own, she had to concentrate on the other two tasks. She sprinted toward their reception area and found a wide-eyed Jean standing at her desk.

"What was that *ka-boom* I heard?" she asked as Nikki rushed in.

Conscious of the people still in the waiting room, looking equally curious, Nikki pulled Jean toward the door. "There's a fire in the hallway leading to the ER," she said tersely. "Send these people outside and call for help, while Lynette and I evacuate the patients from the exam rooms."

With the receiver to her ear, Jean calmly asked the people in the waiting room to move outside. Nikki didn't wait to see if they exited in an orderly fashion as Jean had ordered—she was too busy rushing toward the alarm.

As soon as she pulled the switch and the loud clang started, she hurried through the increasingly smoke-filled hallway in search of her nurse.

She found her in the first room with their appendicitis patient, taking his temperature.

"Sorry to be the bearer of more bad tidings," Nikki said briskly, "but we have to leave the building right now."

Art groaned. "Leave? What for? I just got here."

97

Her gaze met Lynette's. "We have a little bit of a problem."

An announcement came over the loudspeaker. "Code Red. Minor Emergency Center. Code Red. MEC. Attention. This is not a drill. Repeat. This is not a drill."

Art paused. "What's a Code Red?"

"Fire," Nikki said, as the alarm began to clang loud enough to hear through the closed door. "But don't worry. Everything's under control." She hoped. "Can you sit up if we help?"

"I guess I'll have to."

With Nikki taking one arm and Lynette the other, they soon eased Art to a sitting position. He eyed the distance to the door. "I hate to break this to you, but I can't make it."

"Sure you can," Nikki said, although she had her doubts. "Are the other exam rooms occupied?" she asked Lynette.

"I just put folks in two and three."

"Get them out of here," Nikki ordered. "I'll stay with Art. Do we have a wheelchair nearby?"

"I think it's in the med room."

"I'll find it while you take care of the others. Are they ambulatory?"

"Undressed, but ambulatory."

"Slap their clothes back on and move 'em out." She turned to Art. "Can you rest by yourself for a minute until I come back? I promise I'll be quick."

He nodded. "Yeah, sure, but if I don't lie down again, I'll end up on the floor."

She helped him recline, wondering if a wheelchair would be enough to move him to safety. It would have to be. "Hang tight," she told him.

"Can't do anything else," he replied wryly.

Steeling her ears to the deafening noise of the alarm, Nikki dashed into the hallway and rushed toward the med room. No wheelchair. Not sure of where else to look and unwilling to waste time, she retraced her steps, noting that the smoke appeared thicker than it had earlier.

Suddenly she ran into what seemed like a brick wall.

"Galen!" she exclaimed, deciding that he was a sight for her sore, smoke-irritated eyes, even if his grim face and tousled hair made him appear like a specter in the hazy hallway. "What are you doing here?"

Galen grabbed her shoulders as he swept his gaze over her from head to toe, enjoying the feeling of relief that coursed through him. The heavy double fire doors were always closed between his department and the hallway leading to hers, so he hadn't known about the fire until the announcement had come over the loudspeaker. Then his heart had beaten in double time.

"I should be asking you that," he said, more crossly than he'd intended. "You're supposed to be outside with everyone else."

"I'm evacuating our last patient. He needs a wheelchair and I can't find one."

He mumbled a curse. "Maybe we can get by without it."

"I don't think so," she said. "What Art really needs is a gurney. Hot appendix."

"What's he doing in the MEC instead of ER?"

"He complained of a generalized stomachache. I was waiting for the lab results and a phone call from Dr Stevens before I sent him upstairs."

He strode into Art's room. "No wheelchair in sight," he said, sounding unconcerned—although he was. "Can you make it if I support you?"

Art drew his legs up to curl into a fetal position. "Aw, man, I don't think so."

"Can you find a gurney?" Nikki asked. "I hate to jostle him more than we have to."

Galen eyed the young man's form and made an instant decision. "You go and I'll stay. If the situation gets worse, I can sling him over my shoulder and carry him out. You can't."

"I barely know my way around the hospital, much less where I'd find equipment. You're the one who needs to go. Art is *my* patient, so I'm the one who's staying."

The distinct mulish set on her face told him that, short of flinging *her* over his shoulder and carrying her out, she wouldn't leave.

"You're wasting time," she warned.

He shot her a glare, then left. Intending to go around the building to enter the ER through the ambulance bay, he reached the front entrance just as two fire engines and an ambulance pulled into the front driveway. Firemen streamed off their trucks like ants and entered the building. At the same time two paramedics began unloading equipment from the back of their ambulance. One of them was Annie McCall, and while she was a welcome sight, the empty gurney that she and her partner were readying for use was even more so.

He rushed to Annie's side. "Are you using that for anyone in particular?" he demanded without preamble.

Annie guided the gurney to a spot beside the ambulance. "No. Why?"

"I need it." Without giving her or her partner time to argue, he steered it onto the sidewalk and rushed toward the entrance.

"I'm sorry, sir." A policeman in his mid-twenties

stopped him at the visitors' desk. "You can't go any farther."

"The hell I can't!" he exploded. "There's a doctor and an extremely sick man in there and I intend to get them out."

"The fire department will handle it."

Galen gave the officer his most lofty glare. "You can either step aside or end up on this gurney yourself, but I *am* going in."

He didn't budge or appear intimidated. Apparently he'd stood up to tougher characters than Galen before. "I'm sorry, sir, but I have my orders."

"For the love of…" Galen ran a hand through his hair, the only legal way he knew how to release his frustration at the moment.

Annie's voice came from behind. "It's OK, Dave. I'm going with him."

"Sorry, Annie," Officer Dave said. "No one is supposed to go in."

Annie bristled. "Come on, Dave…"

The grizzled fire chief approached, his walkie-talkie in hand. His piercing black eyes raked over the trio as he frowned. "What's the problem here?"

Frustrated by the delay, Galen explained. "We have a doctor inside, tending a patient with a hot appendix. They're at the opposite end of the MEC and need a gurney to get him out."

His walkie-talkie squawked, but Galen couldn't make head or tail of the conversation.

"Ten-four," the chief acknowledged, before he turned to Galen and Annie. "Hurry up," he barked.

Forgoing the thanks so as to not waste another minute, Galen took off, conscious of Annie following. He whizzed through the lobby and careened around the corners, idly deciding that those frowned-upon med-school gurney races were now paying off. The smoke seemed less dense now, which was a good sign.

He flung open the door to Nikki's exam room and pushed the gurney inside. ''Your ride is here, along with reinforcements.''

''It's about time,'' she said cheerfully, giving Annie a nod of acknowledgement.

''Were you worried?''

She shook her head. ''I knew you'd come back.''

His chest swelled after hearing her statement of simple faith. For the first time since their conversation a week ago, he felt as if he was finally making progress, although he didn't want to jinx anything by letting her know how much her comment had touched him.

''You're darn right, I'd be back,'' he said lightly. ''Locums are hard to find.''

''And don't you forget it,'' she retorted with a smile, and turned back to Art. ''Here's the plan,'' she said as Galen and Annie pushed the gurney against the exam table and raised it so the two were at the same height. ''We have to move you from point A to point B. Can you roll over or do we need to lift you?''

''I'll try rolling.''

After careful maneuvering and tugging on everyone's part, Art was safely on the stretcher with the straps secured around him.

''Are we set?'' Galen asked, aware of the sheen of sweat on Art's brow.

Art grimaced. ''Yeah.''

''Then we're off.'' Galen and Annie steered him through the doorway, toward the minor emergency center's exit.

"Easy on the bumps," Nikki said as they came to the metal strip separating the linoleum from the carpeting.

"Yeah." Art clutched his side. "Aw, man, I still can't believe this is happening."

Nikki looked over her shoulder to exchange a smile with Galen. "Your appendix or the fire?"

"Both. I positively hate waiting. I just want this over and done with."

"As soon as we get the all-clear," Galen told him, "you'll have priority treatment."

"Some consolation." Art flung his arm over his face. "The one day I come to the hospital and need surgery is the same day the place burns down."

Nikki chuckled as they passed through the automatic doors and came to a stop under the covered walkway and well out of the path of the entrance. "Just think of how you can use this in your act someday."

He managed a grin. "I'll be sure and take notes."

Outside, Galen eyed the scene of organized chaos, glad that the few clouds in the sky kept the sun from mercilessly beating down on those unfortunate enough not to be under the canopy. Staff members milled around the patients in wheelchairs and on crutches while the more ambulatory patients and visitors simply waited and watched with wide eyes and slack jaws.

"Here's where I leave you," Annie said as she set the brake. "Just don't forget to give my gurney back when you're finished."

Galen grinned. "I won't. And thanks."

"Yell if you need anything else." With that parting remark, Annie returned to her partner's side.

"That worked out well," he commented.

"You stole her stretcher?" Nikki asked.

"Borrowed it," he corrected, seconds before he saw one

of his colleagues standing with a few of the ER nurses.
"And speaking of luck," he told Art, "I see our surgeon
across the way. Have you met him, Nikki?"

"Not yet."

"Then I'll bring him over."

"Yippee," Art said glumly. "Nothing like having a
medical consult in the great outdoors."

Galen strode in Collin Stevens's direction, pulled him
aside and outlined the situation.

The forty-year-old surgeon grinned. "I was just coming
to see him when the alarm went off. I wondered where my
patient ended up."

"He's under the overhang with Dr Lawrence."

"The locum for Tremaine?"

"That's her."

Stevens looked in that direction. "Nice-looking.
Single?"

"Yes, and you're not."

The older man clapped him on the shoulder and laughed.
"This is a switch. Feeling a little territorial, are you?"

"Some," Galen admitted. "We were in residency together."

"Ah," Stevens said, with a knowing lilt to his voice,
"could she possibly be the proverbial one who got away?"

Galen grinned. He hadn't thought of his situation in
those terms before but, now that he did, they were appropriate. "Just check out her patient, will you?"

Stevens guffawed again, then accompanied Galen to
Nikki's side. After the introductions, he became purely
professional. "White count?"

Nikki answered. "Eleven point eight with a definite shift
to the left. Classic rebound tenderness in the lower right
quadrant."

Stevens smiled at his new patient. "As soon as this circus is over, we'll work on fixing what ails you."

Art smiled weakly. "Sounds like a good deal to me."

Just then Galen caught Jean's frantic wave. He excused himself, then joined her and Lynette.

"We overheard the chatter on the walkie-talkie," Jean reported excitedly. "They think this was deliberate."

A cold chill ran down Galen's spine. "Are you sure? Sometimes the static makes it easy to misunderstand." At least, he hoped she'd misunderstood their transmission.

"I'm telling you," Jean insisted. "I distinctly heard them say 'deliberate.' Granted, I didn't hear most of the conversation, but that word came through loud and clear. Dr Lawrence is lucky she wasn't hurt."

"What?" He'd thought she'd been caught up in the excitement like everyone else. He didn't know she'd been more directly involved.

"She was in the hallway when the sparks started flying," Jean said. "She ran back to my office and we got things rolling."

Lynette leaned forward and spoke softly. "You don't suppose this might have something to do with Emma, do you?"

Although he didn't want to think the fire was anything but an accident, their suspicious mood was infectious.

"I hope not," he said fervently.

Nikki listened to Art and Dr Stevens with half an ear, especially after she noticed Galen in an intense conversation with Jean and Lynette.

Determined not to be left out, she excused herself, then picked her way around the television news crew to join them.

"What's wrong?" she asked, glancing from one to the other.

"Jean says she overheard the firemen saying it was deliberate," Galen replied.

She faced her receptionist. "Are you sure?"

"Yes, I am."

An unwelcome thought came to her and she took a step forward. "Emma? I need to check on Emma."

"We will," Galen promised, grabbing her elbow and pinning her to the spot. "They won't let you in."

"I'll find another entrance."

"Just relax until we hear the official word," he said firmly. "Now isn't the time to panic."

A commotion at the entrance drew everyone's attention, especially Nikki's. The firemen, who'd swarmed through the building with set faces and hurried strides earlier, now exited with smiles on their faces and walked at a more normal pace.

The fire chief followed with a veritable entourage, including a man wearing the fire department's uniform but without the protective gear, Hope's CEO, Thomas Waverly, and a police officer. After clearing the automatic doors, the chief stopped.

"You folks can go back inside," he announced. "Everything's under control."

"See?" Galen breathed in her ear. "It can't be that bad. It's hardly been thirty minutes."

Nikki didn't care if it had been ten. Now that Emma's safety had been called into question, she didn't want to waste time popping in to see her.

She brushed past the fire chief, but Thomas Waverly stepped in her path. "Dr Lawrence?" he asked. "Chief Becker would like to talk to you."

Hating the delay, she glanced at Galen and mentally

telegraphed her message. He apparently read her mind because he nodded.

"I'll see you in a few minutes," he promised.

Satisfied that he'd check on Emma, she turned to Chief Becker, praying that this wouldn't take long. "What would you like to know?"

He guided her away from the entrance to make room for the people slowly moving back inside. "This is Bill Thompson, our arson investigator," he said as he glanced at the fireman beside him.

Arson? Jean, their resident find-a-crook-under-every-rock staff member, had been right. Nikki acknowledged the thirtyish blond with a nod.

"I understand you reported the fire, Dr Lawrence," Thompson said.

"My receptionist made the call but, yes, I noticed the smoke first."

"Did you see anything else?"

"Not really. I thought I'd smelled something unusual…like something burning…so I went to investigate. I headed down the hallway, but nothing seemed out of the ordinary."

"Nothing at all?"

"Just someone going into the family room near the ER."

This news made his eyes gleam and her wonder if that person had been responsible. He immediately spoke into his walkie-talkie, instructing the person at the other end to go through the room she'd mentioned with a fine-toothed comb.

As soon as he'd finished, he addressed her again. "Can you identify this person?"

"I wish I could," she apologized, "but I really only saw the door closing. I'd turned around to go back when

I heard several loud pops and saw a flash of sparks out of the corner of my eye.''

"Then what?''

She shrugged. "Lots of white smoke.''

"Did you notice anything on the floor?''

She pictured the scene again. She'd been looking up, not down. "No. I'm sorry.''

Thompson smiled. "Thank you, Doctor. You've been very helpful.''

"Then…'' She paused. "It wasn't electrical?''

He shook his head and held out his hand. Inside rested a plastic bag containing remnants of string and the burned-out shells of something she hadn't seen since she was a kid.

"Nothing electrical,'' he said. "Just a string of old-fashioned smoke bombs and firecrackers.''

After finding Emma snoozing contentedly in one of the day-care cribs, Galen thanked Susan for letting him interrupt.

"Drop in any time,'' she assured him.

Grateful to report good news, Galen returned to the MEC with what he liked to refer to as "deliberate speed.''

"She isn't back yet,'' Jean reported as soon as he poked his head into her office. "I assume she's still talking to the fire chief.''

"Thanks.'' He strode back through the front lobby in time to meet Nikki.

"Emma is sleeping like a baby,'' he said with a smile. "Susan said everything there has been quiet, unless you count one young man who threw a temper tantrum because he didn't like his snack.''

"That's good to know, but she wasn't in any danger,'' Nikki told him.

''The fire?''

''Someone decided to shoot off a few firecrackers and smoke bombs.''

''Who?''

''I don't know the kid's name, but after I told them I'd seen the door to the family room just off the ER close right before it happened, a few firemen went inside to look for clues. They found him sitting in the corner.''

''Maybe he was just waiting for someone to rescue him.''

''With a pile of matches and more firecrackers beside him?'' She shook her head. ''I don't think so and neither did the police.''

''I wonder why anyone would do such a thing,'' he mused aloud.

She looked away to the group coming toward them. ''It's hard to say. I'll bet this is our culprit.''

Galen watched the young dark-haired boy stoically walk out between two police officers. Recognition was immediate, along with horrified surprise. ''I know that kid. That's Walt's son.''

''Walt who?''

''Walt Whittaker. He's the physician who was killed in the same plane crash that injured Jared Tremaine. I'd heard that Robbie was having a hard time dealing with the accident, but for him to do this…'' He shook his head. ''Poor Julia.''

''He's obviously a troubled young man.''

''Yeah.'' He grew thoughtful. ''I haven't kept in contact with the family since Walt's funeral like I should have. Maybe Robbie's smoke-bomb incident is his way of demanding attention from his father's cronies.''

''Or maybe he just has a lot of anger at the world bottled up inside,'' she said. ''It has to come out in some form.

He's just lucky that he didn't start a real fire. This place has so many flammables that a stray spark could have devastating consequences.''

''A fact which the police and his mother will emphasize most emphatically, I'm sure,'' he said, saddened to see his colleague's son being guided into the back of the police cruiser.

''And speaking of consequences,'' Nikki began, ''I suppose my department is under water.''

He grinned. ''Did you forget your swim fins?''

''Along with my scuba gear and inner tube.''

''Don't worry. When I breezed through a few minutes ago, looking for you, the housekeeping staff were already hard at work.''

''Then I suppose we should be, too.''

''How about dinner tonight?''

''It depends on what you're hungry for.''

''The Red Pagoda has a great buffet if you like oriental.''

''OK. What time should Emma and I be ready?''

''I was hoping we could leave her at home,'' he said slowly, watching her reaction.

''She's a little too young to stay by herself, Galen.''

He rolled his eyes. ''I know that. I thought we could find a sitter.''

''Not at this time. Besides, I wouldn't feel right leaving her with another stranger so soon after I got her.''

He hadn't expected her to jump at the opportunity to go out with him on what he considered a date, but hope had still sprung eternal.

''What time will Miss Piglet be ready for a night on the town?'' he asked, trying to hide his disappointment.

''Around eight.''

''I'll be there at seven, right after I get off work.''

"What for?"

"To help you. If she's awake, she'll need someone to keep her occupied so you can do whatever primping you women think you need to do."

"Primping? I'll have you know that I do *not* primp."

"I stand corrected. I'll see you at seven."

He headed off, then stopped short when she called his name.

"Yeah?" he acknowledged.

"Do you still want to go out to dinner without Emma some time?"

Did birds fly? Did dogs bark? Was she the cause of his sleepless nights? Yes, yes, and *yes*.

"I wouldn't have asked if it wasn't what I wanted." He focused a steady gaze on hers, willing her to see his sincerity.

"How does Friday night sound? I could probably find a babysitter by then. That is, if you're interested. Maybe we could even go to a movie?"

"Interested? Of course, I am."

Her face colored as if she'd seen the hunger he felt. "Friday night it is."

Without another word she hurried off, leaving him to realize that he'd just received an unexpected blessing.

Four days seemed an interminably long time but, as he'd once been told, good things came to those who waited.

Eager for their evening outing, Nikki went to the day-care center to gather up Emma and her belongings. Instead of finding the usually placid baby, she found Susan pacing the floor with a fussy and clearly inconsolable Emma.

"She's been like this for the last two hours," Susan said, handing her over quite quickly and with apparent relief. "We've tried everything and the only thing that works to some degree is to keep her moving. Preferably, bouncing.''

''What's the matter, Em?'' Nikki asked the infant perched on her shoulder. ''Do you have a tummyache?''

Emma's lower lip quivered and huge tears brimmed in her eyes as she let out another whimper.

''Shall we go home and play in the tub for a little while?'' Nikki asked, knowing how much the baby enjoyed the water.

''We checked her temp and she's not running a fever so, whatever it is, it's probably minor,'' Susan added. ''Which is why I didn't call you.''

''That's fine. I'm just sorry she made your last hour miserable.''

Susan laughed. ''That's what's nice about providing day care. You can enjoy the little ones and when they get fussy give them back to their parents. It's the best of both worlds.''

Emma let out a half-wail, as if bored with being in one place for so long. ''I'd better go,'' Nikki said.

''See you tomorrow.''

Emma roared her unhappiness during the ride home, forcing Nikki to close her ears. Her hope that the motion of the car would soothe the infant came to nothing. A watery romp in the baby bathtub didn't improve her disposition, neither did a trip to the balcony to listen to the wind chimes. For the first time while in Nikki's care, Emma turned her face away from a bottle.

The only thing that seemed to help was for Nikki to carry her in a football hold and to walk around the room. She lost track of time until the doorbell rang.

''You're early,'' she told Galen as soon as she opened the door and let him in.

''Nothing better to do.''

She bounced the baby on her hip. "We're going to have to make other plans for tonight."

"What's wrong?"

"Emma has a tummyache. There's no way I'm taking her out in public when she's feeling wretched and will make everyone else equally as miserable."

Emma snuffled in Nikki's arm and kicked her legs.

Galen bent over to peer into her face. "Hey, Miss Piglet, what's all the fuss about?" He reached out to take her from Nikki. "I'll take over. Go do whatever you need to do."

"She'll get us kicked out of the restaurant," Nikki warned, still feeling the touch of his fingers as they'd brushed across her midriff.

"Just get ready," he said as he ambled across the room. "It isn't as if we have reservations to worry about."

She hesitated. "Are you sure?"

"Go."

She went. She showered in record time and jumped into a pair of red and white floral capri pants and a red tank top. Suddenly aware of the quiet, she hurried out of her bedroom and saw Galen and a now-contented Emma sitting on the balcony in the shade of the roof's overhang.

"How did you do that?" she asked, amazed and somewhat irritated that he'd accomplished what she could not.

He grinned. "Trade secret."

"Seriously."

"How do I know? I just held her and we talked about what ailed her, what she wanted out of life, how to handle boys. Important stuff."

"How to handle boys?"

"Can't have these discussions too soon," he said cheerfully. "She took in every word."

"I'll bet." What was it about Galen that a few minutes

with him made women, including the three-month-old variety, turn into domesticated pussycats? "Where have you gotten all your baby experience?"

He shrugged. "Who said I had any?"

"Believe me. Most men who haven't been surrounded with relatives' children run in the opposite direction when a baby appears. With five brothers, I know what I'm talking about."

"It's really not that big a deal," he said. "I helped out for a few weeks in the NICU when they were short of cuddlers for the babies."

She stared at him in surprise. "You did? You never said anything."

"It was only temporary and I didn't think it was important."

A man who willingly cuddled babies? What woman wouldn't want him on that basis alone?

"It contradicted your playboy image, didn't it?" she guessed.

"A little and, as I said, it was only for a few weeks and not worth mentioning." His tone changed. "Are you ready to go? Emma has assured me that she'll be on her best behavior."

Nikki wasn't quite convinced of Emma's co-operation but, after seeing the former bundle of energy lie quietly on Galen's shoulder as she gazed at her surroundings, she could almost believe it.

"Not quite. Jean thinks we'll be on tonight's six o'clock newscast, so I want to see if one of us happened to be a momentary movie star."

"I'll be in as soon as I pry myself out of the chair."

Back in the living room, Nikki clicked on the television with her remote just as the announcer began his teaser and the camera flashed a scene with a fire truck parked in front of the hospital.

"Top local stories include a reported fire at Hope City Memorial, the County Fair opens this weekend, and the City Council is considering incentives to curb water usage. Stay tuned for these and other stories. But first, our national news…"

"We were mentioned," she remarked as Galen walked inside. "They only showed one picture, though."

"Maybe they'll show more during the broadcast."

"I hope so. Jean will be so thrilled."

Nikki turned back to the television, intending to shut it off, when the announcer's story caught her attention.

"The trial of casino owner Ralph Arches is slated to begin next month in Emerson County, Oklahoma after several long delays…"

"I heard about this guy," Nikki exclaimed, recognizing the picture of the accused on the screen. "His story has been in all the national newspapers."

"I must have missed it. What did he do?"

"Hired someone to murder his wife a year ago and then billed the amount to his corporate account as a business expense."

"Sounds like a nice guy."

She focused on the newscast. "Shh."

"The chief witness is reportedly the company's accountant who noticed the discrepancy during a routine audit. A grand jury indicted Arches on his testimony and, because of feared mob connections, the man and his family are in protective custody…"

Another picture flashed onto the screen, this time showing the courtroom scene as Arches was led away following his indictment. Near the bottom of the image, Nikki caught a glimpse of someone who suddenly set her hair on end.

A gray-haired man stood with his back to the camera while he leaned heavily on a woman's arm. A dark-haired woman.

The woman she'd met once before and for only a few minutes.

Emma's mother.

CHAPTER SEVEN

"OHMIGOSH. Did you see her?" Nikki exclaimed, pointing to the screen.

"See who?" Galen asked as he rubbed Emma's back.

"The woman near the bottom of the picture."

"What woman?"

The announcer moved on to the next story and the image changed. "You missed her. Darn it, I wish I had this on videotape."

"Missed who?" he demanded. "Come on, Nik. You aren't making any sense."

"You missed seeing Emma's mother." She started to pace. "This is absolutely amazing."

"How can you be so positive?" he asked. "The picture was on the screen less than five seconds."

"It's her," she insisted. "Don't you believe me?"

"Let's say that I don't *dis*believe you. If you think she looked like the woman who claimed to be Emma's mother, then who am I to argue?" He grew thoughtful. "If you're right—"

"I am."

"Then that would explain the secrecy involved." He gently stroked Emma's head. "But not why she dumped Emma on you."

"Maybe she was afraid I'd refuse."

"She gave you that option in her letter," he reminded her.

None of those excuses fully explained what had happened and Nikki knew that. She sensed that perhaps there

117

was something else going on, something else that wasn't obvious, but what that might be she wouldn't know until Alice returned for her daughter.

"I'm a trauma physician, not a psychoanalyst or a criminal profiler," she said impatiently. "I'm simply trying to give the woman the benefit of the doubt. It isn't as if she simply dumped her and ran. She tied everything up nice and legal."

"Legal papers or not, her actions were still irresponsible," he said flatly. "Not to mention how they also raise the question of why she chose Hope in the first place. Or why she didn't keep Emma with her if they were in protective custody."

"Maybe she wanted a place where the trial wouldn't be big news? And perhaps the town's name made it seem like the perfect place to stash her daughter for safekeeping. Protective custody doesn't come with any guarantees."

"No," he agreed. "But none of your theories explain why she chose you."

"Some things we'll simply have to wait to figure out when the time comes. If I'm right, we'll be seeing Alice Martin the day Arches is convicted."

"Time will tell." Galen's skepticism was obvious, but Nikki didn't feel like arguing with him over something that she couldn't prove.

"And," he added, with a broad grin, "if you're right, I'll even let you gloat with an 'I told you so.'"

She laughed. "It's a deal."

"And speaking of time, Emma's been quiet. Is she asleep?"

Emma's head was turned away from Galen, so Nikki peered around him to check. "Out for the count," she whispered, stroking the fine wisps of hair off her tiny forehead. "Are you sure you didn't drug her?"

"Only with my charming personality. I send out extremely calm, relaxed vibes, or haven't you noticed?"

"Not at all," she lied. "Then you're used to women falling asleep in your arms?"

"Only those with special invitations." His mouth curled into a wide smile. "Want one?"

Yes, she wanted to say. *But only if I get the last one you're issuing.*

"On second thought, I rescind my offer," he said.

The seeds of rejection started to sprout, but before she could marshal her thoughts and form a witty retort, he shook her equilibrium again.

"When you're in my arms—" his voice sounded as smooth as melted chocolate and sinfully sexy "—we won't be sleeping."

Galen watched Nikki's thoughts flit across her face, thoughts that ranged first from jealousy to disappointment and finally to embarrassed surprise. In hindsight, he wondered how he'd misread her so completely during those years of residency. Then again, it was easy to miss what one wasn't looking for and he'd been too certain of his unsuitability to let himself dream.

Now he dreamed all the time.

Seeing that he'd thoroughly rattled Nikki's composure, he would have liked to have demonstrated what he intended with her in his arms, but holding a baby made it impossible. "Where do you want me to lay her?"

Nikki's mouth closed with a sudden snap as if she suddenly remembered the third party in this scene. "I was going to suggest her crib because she's so worn out, but that means we can't go…"

The dismay on her face nearly made him smile. Somehow he doubted if the idea of postponing dinner or skipping it entirely had caused her reaction. Most likely, it was the realization that they would be, for all intents and purposes, alone in her apartment. She would finally have to address those issues concerning him that she'd been avoiding and make a decision.

From the hesitation on her face he doubted if now was a good time to forge ahead. For tonight, and in case she'd forgotten, it was enough for her to know that those platonic touches were only a prelude to what he really wanted.

It would also give her something to think about until their official date on Friday.

He shrugged, opting for a nonchalant attitude when he was already planning his strategy for the upcoming days. "I don't mind. I'm flexible."

She led him into the spare bedroom and, as soon as he'd placed Emma on her back in her crib, covered her with a light blanket. Shooing him from the room, she followed and left the door slightly ajar.

If he hadn't craved being in her company so much, he would have done the gentlemanly thing and offered to leave, but he looked forward to their evenings together and so he couldn't.

"How long do you think she'll sleep?" he asked instead.

"It's hard to say. Susan said she'd been fussy for a while, so Emma has either worn herself out and will sleep for hours, or this is just a temporary lull."

She bit her lip in obvious indecision. "Galen…" she began slowly, using the tone of voice that didn't bode well for the listener.

He steeled himself to hear the worst. "I'm sorry if I spoke too soon, but I won't apologize for wanting it. For wanting you."

"You don't have to apologize," she said softly. "I'm flattered."

Relief…and pure masculine satisfaction swelled in his chest. "Then you aren't going to throw me out on my ear?"

"I should." She softened her comment with a smile. "But it would require more energy than I have."

"So what do you want to do?" He was curious, but didn't want to appear over-eager when in fact, he was.

"Honestly?"

"I wouldn't have asked if I didn't want to know."

"Order a pizza with extra mushrooms, pop in a movie, put my feet up and let my hair down."

He eyed her hair, still pulled away from her face and held at the back of her head with a clip. Her wish didn't quite mesh with his, but he could afford to be patient. Besides, she had been through a rough day. When they made love, he didn't want her to be physically exhausted before they started.

"I think we can handle all of the above," he said.

While she channel-surfed, he took care of ordering the deluxe pizza that she requested, although he hated vegetables on his pizza and intended to pick them off.

When he joined her on the sofa, he brought her cherry-flavored cola and his Dr Pepper soft drink.

"Thanks," she said, taking the glass. "You shouldn't have."

"I was in the kitchen anyway. So, what are we watching?"

"Nothing yet. The next movie doesn't start for twenty minutes."

He sat beside her, noticing that she'd unclipped her hair and smelled of gardenias and baby powder.

Maybe he should have left after all.

"I talked to Julia Whittaker this afternoon," he commented, determined to think of something other than Nikki's perfectly kissable mouth.

"I bet she was devastated to hear about her son."

"Yeah. She was crushed. He's at home, but he just made himself a part of the legal system."

"Juvenile detention?"

"Probably not, but he'll end up on some sort of probation. The juvenile judge is a proponent of community service, so he'll most likely have something to do along those lines."

"Counseling?"

"Definitely."

"I hope it helps."

"I do, too." He stretched his left arm along the top of the sofa, behind her back, as he made himself comfortable. "The only problem is, once he's in the system, they'll dog his steps for a long time."

She shifted positions. "Speaking of being in the system, I can understand why Mrs Martin prepared all the paperwork for Emma. If she'd just left her, Emma would have ended up in foster-care and she might never have gotten her back."

"True. But I'm curious…you never did explain why you agreed to her scheme when you didn't know the woman."

"I thought I did." She spoke lightly, but he'd felt her stiffen.

"You said that you didn't want Emma to be passed around like a package, but you didn't explain why you thought she would be. It doesn't really matter one way or another to me, because your decision just proves how kind and generous you are." He grinned. "Just like Cal warned me."

"Why is it that the men in my family are the only ones

who make kindness appear as a negative trait rather than a positive one?''

"Because you have a tendency to over-extend yourself. You might be this tough-as-nails ER doc, but underneath that armor you're pure marshmallow.''

She poked him in the ribs. "I am not.''

"OK. Then explain to me why you kept Emma when you didn't have to.'' He narrowed his eyes. "Or is that part of the secret?''

He heard her slight hesitation. "It's not a secret,'' she said. "At least, it doesn't have anything to do with Emma's situation.''

"Oh?''

"You probably don't know that I was adopted.''

Hating to see her fingers clenched together, he slid his hand between hers until she was holding his hand rather than her own. "No. Lots of people are adopted. It's no big deal.''

"I was ten when I went to live with the Lawrences. I was so scared of everyone. They were all so much bigger than I was. It took me a while to get used to being in a houseful of rowdy boys.''

He pictured her at that age, small, elfin, and probably as cute as any little girl could hope to be. "I can imagine.''

"Then you didn't have any other siblings before you moved in with your adoptive family?''

She shook her head. "If I did, my mother probably got rid of them the same way she did me.''

A warning flag began to fly. "What do you mean?''

"She left me on the steps of the Catholic church like a piece of unwanted luggage on my eighth birthday.''

Galen had asked for the truth, but he hadn't expected this sort of revelation. "I'm so sorry.''

"Don't be,'' she said kindly. "I spent the next two years

in foster-care until the Lawrences took me. I know that Emma's situation isn't like mine, but I couldn't pass her to the next person on Mrs Martin's list like she was simply a box being delivered.''

"Did you realize you were being abandoned at the church?"

"No. She said she'd come back, but she never did."

He suspected that the pain might have faded, but from her far-away expression the memory had not.

"Maybe she couldn't."

She shook her head. "When the authorities found her, she immediately signed relinquishment papers so she wouldn't be prosecuted for endangerment of a child. Which makes her promise to me rather empty, wouldn't you agree?"

"I'm sorry," he repeated.

"Don't be." She shrugged. "If I'd stayed with her, I wouldn't be where I am today. Becoming part of the Lawrence family was the best thing that could have happened."

"No wonder they're over-protective of you."

Nikki smiled. "I don't know how I would have managed if not for them. I can't tell you how many times the boys got in a fight because someone teased me."

"Defending your honor?"

"They were my guardian angels," she said simply. "As time went on, they taught me to defend myself, but it didn't stop them from smoothing the way for me whenever they could. Which is how Cal got involved when I went off to residency. Of course, I didn't mind knowing that we were connected in some small way through my cousin."

And he'd blown his opportunity. He was lucky she hadn't told her brothers that the two of them had made it to third base that night and had been on their way to home plate or he'd be wearing dentures and walking with a permanent limp.

"Do you ever hear from your mother? Your birth mother, that is?"

"I saw her two years later in passing. When I was twelve, we got word that she'd overdosed." She squeezed his hand. "And now you know why I kept Emma. I couldn't *not* take her."

The summary of her early childhood explained so much. He understood why she'd been so hurt by his honorable intentions and why she didn't believe his sudden change of heart. If she'd learned not to trust her own mother's promises, then she wouldn't give her trust easily to anyone.

He'd lost far more that night than he'd realized. Regaining the ground wouldn't be as easy the second time around, but if her brothers had earned her faith and adoration, then there was hope for him to succeed as well. It would simply take time.

"If you run through our patients this fast every day at the same time you're helping with ER," Lynette told Nikki on Friday, "they're never going to believe that we need more than two physicians to staff our emergency department."

"Sorry," Nikki said, unrepentant. "I just want to get out of here on time."

"Big plans for the weekend?"

"Just for tonight," she admitted. "Galen and I are going to dinner and a movie."

"With Emma?"

Nikki grinned. "I splurged and found a sitter."

"Ah, that explains everything. Have a good time."

"I will." She'd been eagerly anticipating this evening ever since the beginning of the week. After spilling her family history, she'd felt remarkably light, as if the weight of the world had lifted from her shoulders. If Galen had been worried about not being "worthy", her story should have disabused him of that notion.

"I don't mean to be speaking out of turn, but…" Lynette hesitated.

"What is it?"

"When he first came, he earned somewhat of a reputation with the ladies, if you know what I mean."

"Oh, yes," she answered wryly. "I do."

"The sad thing is, Dr Stafford doesn't deserve a word of it."

Yeah, right. And I'm related to the royal family! "What makes you say that?"

"I know he went out with a different woman every few weeks, but my George was considered a playboy, too, in his day. Trust me when I say that Dr Stafford hasn't come anywhere near George's exploits."

Nikki had met the balding, pudgy George and, while he'd been quite personable and talkative, if he'd been the footloose character his wife claimed, then marriage had definitely changed him.

"Anyway," Lynette continued, "several months ago, Dr Stafford more or less dropped out of circulation. Regardless of his history and for what my opinion's worth, I think he's a lot like George. Once he settles down with the right woman, he won't stray."

Lynette's subtle hint wasn't so subtle, but Nikki knew that the nurse thought the sun rose and set on Galen. It wasn't any surprise. When her husband had suffered a heart attack, Galen had administered the clot-busting drug that had saved his life. As far as she was concerned, Galen could do no wrong.

"What exactly are you trying to say?"

"Don't let the rumors influence you," Lynette said, "in case you're having trouble deciding if he's the right one or not."

"I'll keep your endorsement in mind if we should get to that point."

But as she soaked in the tub and got ready for Galen and the babysitter to arrive that evening, she knew she was approaching that very point at light speed.

Galen had made his intention known on Monday night. To say that she didn't want the same would be a lie, because she wanted him, too.

Desperately.

"The question is," she told Emma, who was lying in the middle of her double bed while Nikki got dressed, "when my contract ends, can I walk away from him without being crushed a second time?"

Emma gurgled.

"I know, I know. He said he was ready to settle down, but what guarantee do I have that he won't grow tired of me? I'm nothing at all like the women he's dated." She eyed her frame in the full-length mirror screwed onto the closet door.

"I'm short and remarkably average. He prefers tall and beautiful."

Emma grunted.

"It's true," she added. "I've seen enough of them to know. If we hadn't gone through residency together, and if he hadn't been friends with Cal, Galen wouldn't have given me a second thought."

Emma dropped her chew toy and yelled her displeasure until Nikki placed it back in her little hand.

"He might seem laid-back, but he's a hunter," she informed her. "Once he catches a girl, it doesn't take him long to lose interest."

Why not enjoy what he's offering? her little voice taunted. *You know you want it. You have for a very long time.*

"It would be one way to know if he's sincere or not," she mused aloud to Emma. "I'd either last longer than the others, or I wouldn't, but I wouldn't be in limbo. And I know him well enough to recognize the signs of boredom. Wouldn't it be better to see that before I give up my locum job?

"But can I survive if my love isn't enough to hold him?" she asked, wishing Emma could answer. "I'm afraid that once I take this final step and things don't work out, no one else will ever compare."

But none do now, do they?

Stunned by her realization, Nikki sank onto the bed. Subconsciously she'd known that, which was why she didn't bother dating and why she'd been determined after her trip to Hope to put Galen completely from her mind. She might use the excuse that she didn't want a long-distance relationship, but the truth was painfully clear. Galen simply outshone every man she'd ever met.

"Tell me, Em, what should I do?"

Emma waved her arms in the air.

"You're right," she said, as she rose to spritz herself with perfume. "I'll play it by ear. Things like this can't be decided or planned ahead of time. I made that mistake once before. I won't do it again."

Then what was this evening's emergency trip to the drugstore for?

Wishful thinking, she told her little voice loftily. Whatever happened would just…happen. And when it did, she simply wanted to be prepared.

She gathered Emma off the bed, and waited in the living room for her guests.

Fortunately, the sitter arrived a few minutes later and the opportunity to debate her alternatives passed. By the time she'd outlined her instructions to the sixty-five-year-old woman who lived on the first floor, Galen walked into her apartment.

"If you have any problems," she told Ruby, "don't hesitate to call. You have the number."

"I won't," Ruby replied, holding Emma with an ease that spoke of her extensive grandmotherly experience. "Have fun."

As the door closed behind her, Nikki hesitated.

Galen grabbed her arm and led her into the elevator. "Come on. Ruby seems to know what she's doing."

"Why do I feel as if I'm doing something I shouldn't?" Nikki complained on the way down to his parked car.

"Spoken like a true mother leaving her infant for the first time. Emma will be fine. If Ruby has a problem, we're only five minutes away."

"I suppose."

"Now, Nik," he chided gently, "this is our date, remember? Just you and me. No one else."

How had she forgotten? This was the moment she'd been waiting for and had dreamed about since their days at St Luke's. It was a time when she could finally shake free of the constraints she'd placed on herself and see him as more than just a friend and colleague. It was also her opportunity to show him the woman underneath the lab coat and medical degree.

"You're right." She smiled up at him as she threaded her arm through his. "For the next three hours, it's just the two of us."

"If we only have three hours, I don't want to waste a minute of it."

As far as Nikki was concerned, they filled each second

to the brim. Galen took her to dinner at a private club where a single rose and candle taper decorated each white linen-covered table and a string quartet played softly in the background.

She glanced around the room at the other patrons. ''I'm underdressed,'' she whispered across the table, conscious of her khaki skirt and plain light blue sweater in comparison to the other women's elegant black skirts and beaded tops. ''You should have warned me.''

He ran his gaze over the crowd. ''Underdressed? I don't think so. They're showing more skin than you are.''

''You know what I mean.''

He raised his wine glass in a toast. ''To the most beautiful woman here.''

His appreciative gaze warmed her down to her toes. ''Thank you.''

Over dinner, the conversation flowed easily as Galen regaled her with stories about his career in Seattle while she shared the details of the places she'd worked. She was almost disappointed to break the spiritual connection when he'd announced it was time to go if they wanted to catch the movie.

Nikki almost suggested that they save it for another time, but as soon as the theater turned dark and he lifted the arm rest between them to tuck her under his arm, she was glad she hadn't.

She'd never been as aware of him as she was during those ninety minutes. Every move, every rustle of his shirt, every brush of his arm against her, every place his finger touched became indelibly marked on her memory.

She closed her eyes and simply let herself feel his solid presence beside her and breathe in the scent that was so uniquely his. If she could have made time stand still, she would have done so without a qualm.

Later, while he drove toward her apartment—she noticed how well he stayed under the speed limit—she let out a sigh.

"Tired?" he asked.

"No. Disappointed our date is over."

"There's always next Friday night."

An entire week away, she wanted to protest. "That's true."

"It isn't as if we won't see each other in the meantime," he commented. "I spend as much time here as I do at my place."

"Speaking of which," she said, turning to face him, "when *are* you going to show us your apartment?"

"After I'm home long enough to clean it."

"Tsk, tsk," she teased. "Do you mean to tell me you've picked up bad housekeeping habits?"

"Domestically challenged is the politically correct word these days."

"I stand corrected. But if we're interfering with your chores, maybe you shouldn't come over one night so you can clean."

"Not a chance. I'll live with the dust."

He parked in a bay near the entrance of her building. "Here we are. Right on time."

"I suppose we should go in and find out how those two managed together."

"I'll walk you up before I leave."

It had been an unwritten rule that he left by ten, out of respect for Emma's bedtime. Right now Nikki wanted to extend their unspoken curfew, even if only for a few more minutes.

A few minutes later he unlocked the door and they quietly slipped inside to find the lights dimmed and Ruby watching television.

"Hi," she said softly, clicking off the television as she rose.

"How did things go?" Nikki asked.

"Great. She's the sweetest baby. One of the best I've ever watched."

Nikki chuckled. "She has her days," she said, thinking of the episode earlier in the week.

"If she sleeps later than usual, don't worry," Ruby said with a sheepish smile. "We were playing and I lost track of time so she didn't go to sleep until about an hour ago."

"As long as everything went well, I don't mind."

Ruby gathered her things, promised to return next week, and left a few minutes later while Nikki peeked in on Emma.

"She's fast asleep," she said when she rejoined Galen in the living room.

"I guess this means I should go, too."

Nikki suddenly felt like Cinderella, who knew she should be leaving and couldn't. Being in similar shoes, she understood why Cinderella had lost her slipper. She'd simply been squeezing every last second out of her evening.

Nikki thought fast. "Are you hungry? How about a scoop of ice cream before you leave?"

He stepped closer, his heavy-lidded gaze trailing over her. "Ice cream is good on a hot night like tonight."

She nodded numbly, conscious of his mouth hovering dangerously close to hers.

"I'd rather taste something sweeter, though."

His breath brushed across the bridge of her nose and forced her own lungs to struggle in their simple task of moving air. "What would that be?" she managed to choke out in a hoarse voice.

"I'll show you."

He pulled her close and took her mouth in one smooth

action that left her reeling from the bolt of lightning that shot from head to toe.

She'd wanted him to kiss her like this, to kiss her until she was mindless of everything but him, and the reality of it exceeded what her imagination had conjured up. If there'd been a meter for intensity, the reading would have sailed off the scale into infinity.

He stopped abruptly, but his hold didn't slacken. For several long moments he simply stared at her, his face wreathed in shadows as he waited silently.

Nikki studied his ruggedly handsome features, hoping to find some flaw, some detail that would cause her common sense to override the yearnings of her heart. She found none.

Instead, she saw something in his expression that was a combination of fierce desire and awed appreciation. His eyes remained steady, the contours of his face unchanged in the space of those heartbeats. He didn't smile, didn't say word, and she sensed that he wouldn't. He'd argued his case and now the decision rested solely upon her shoulders. Like a man who was waiting for sentence to be passed, he simply…waited, hoping for the best and preparing for the worst.

Logic demanded that she look before she leapt, weighed the consequences of impulsive actions. Her spirit begged otherwise.

She hadn't realized until that moment how hard it must have been for him to walk away a year ago because refusing the unspoken question shining out of his eyes required a strength she didn't possess.

Perhaps he'd changed, as he'd said, and perhaps he hadn't, but weren't some things in life worth the risk?

"You offered an invitation to me a few nights ago," she began slowly. "Is it still good?"

"Indefinitely."

"Then I accept."

"I'll spend the entire night," he warned.

"I wouldn't have it any other way."

CHAPTER EIGHT

ONCE those small details had been addressed, nothing else mattered but Nikki's feelings for the man in the room. Galen drew her into his arms again and she went without hesitation. His touch was electrifying as he slipped his fingers underneath the hem of her sweater and anchored her close.

"The lights," she muttered against his mouth, as eager to feel his hands on her bare skin as he obviously was. "And I need to lock the door."

He grunted, presumably in agreement, before he broke contact. Pulling her behind him, he strode across the room to flick the light switch and throw the deadbolt.

Knowing his night vision hadn't adjusted enough to see his way through her apartment, Nikki brushed past him to lead the way into her bedroom. She intended to turn on the small lamp beside the four-poster bed, but he grabbed her arm before she touched the knob.

"Wait."

She straightened. Had he changed his mind again? If he had, she was going to throttle him for bringing her to this state of heightened arousal without giving her relief. "Wait?" she asked, incredulous. "Why?"

He touched the front closure of her sweater and freed three more buttons. "I want to see you covered only in moonlight," he murmured.

Moonlight? She hadn't thought of that, but now that he'd mentioned it... She hadn't closed the curtains or the window when she'd gotten ready for her big evening. Now nothing stopped the moon's glow from softly illuminating the room or held back the light breeze of night air.

"Oh. I thought…" She bit back her sentence, deeming it inconsequential under the circumstances as he completely unbuttoned her shirt and tugged it off her arms

"You thought what?" he asked, his eyes wide and dark as he focused unwaveringly on hers.

"Never mind."

He studied her with the same intensity he used when examining a challenging patient's history. "Did you think I would stop again?"

It didn't seem appropriate to be anything but honest. "Yes."

"I won't," he promised as he pulled both bra straps off her shoulders. "Not this time."

An instant later, she was completely naked to his gaze. "So beautiful," he murmured as he reached out to touch her.

Suddenly she wanted to see him, too. She tugged his shirt out of his chinos and worked the clasp of his belt with more determination than skill, until he finally came to her rescue and took care of it himself.

She reached for his zipper, but he closed one hand around her wrist. "If you want this to be slow and easy…"

She didn't let him finish. "Who said I did? We've wasted too much time as it is."

"We have, haven't we?"

"Not only that," she said, turning on a seductive smile, "slow and easy can come later. Much later."

By mutual agreement, patience had ceased being an option. Instantly the rest of their clothes flew in every direction. Nikki didn't know whose hands undid what, but she didn't care. Only the end result mattered, that they were going to share *the* most beautifully intimate experience that two people could share.

In one smooth movement, he lowered her onto the bed. His head hovered near hers, his mouth only a breath away, when, once again, he froze.

She wanted to pound her fist against the mattress in frustration. ''What now?''

''This isn't the night your brothers call, is it?''

''No, but even if it was, they can leave a message.''

He relaxed, then mumbled as he trailed kisses over her face, ''Good. I don't want any interruptions.''

Nikki wanted to accuse him of doing a rather effective job all by himself, but chiding him for it would only prolong the delay that was already driving her mad. She didn't want to say or do anything that would interfere with upcoming events.

Instantly, a mental image of one big—actually, only about fourteen pounds' worth—interference flashed into her head.

She stiffened. ''Emma.''

Galen raised his head to listen. ''I don't hear her.''

''No. But she's in the other room. Maybe we shouldn't be doing this…''

''Emma isn't going to care,'' he mumbled as he returned to blazing a trail of kisses down her neck. ''And if her real parents were here instead of us, how do you suppose they'd manage to give her brothers and sisters?''

He nibbled on a sensitive spot at the base of her throat and she melted. ''You're right.''

''Of course, I am. And if they need each other the way I need you right now, Emma will some day come from an extremely large family.''

Then, before she could say a word, he started to work

his unique brand of magic and Nikki forgot about everyone and everything except the man beside her.

Galen might tease her about being a wren, but for the first time in her life she soared with the eagles.

The next few weeks passed by in a haze of happiness. Before, she'd always marked the passage of time with each new locum job, but now she had a different standard. She had Emma to use as her clock…her first giggle, the first time she held onto her rattle a full minute without losing it, the first time she blew bubbles.

And Galen? He'd become as much a part of her routine as Emma. He'd slipped into her life as easily as he had when they'd been residents, and on those nights when she lay in bed alone, she wondered what would happen when her contract ended. As far as she knew, Hope didn't have any plans to add an extra ER physician to their staff, even though it was obvious that they could use one.

All of which meant that she'd have to return to her locum assignments. She couldn't afford not to with her medical school debts looming over her head. The thought of only seeing Galen every few weeks and carrying on a courtship via the telephone wasn't a happy one, but it was better than the alternative of not seeing him at all.

No matter what happened in the days ahead, he was a part of her life now. Although she'd tried to tell herself not to get too close—just in case—her heart hadn't listened. A single touch or a mere glance was enough to melt away all resistance and send her pulse into a full gallop.

It wasn't just the physical side of their relationship that kept her enthralled. She simply enjoyed spending time with Galen. He made her laugh and look forward to the experiences of a new day. The thing she'd missed most was the way they discussed their patients and gave each other different perspectives when they were needed. Most importantly, she felt safe in his presence, which probably wasn't a smart thing under the circumstances.

Nikki didn't know what she'd do if she started to count on him and he walked away. The longest he'd ever dated a woman had been five weeks and they would reach that milestone in a few days. She'd told herself not to care one way or another, that she would survive just as she'd survived her mother's abandonment. Today was a gift and therefore this time was what counted. She'd let the future take care of itself.

It looked rather bleak without him, though.

It also looked rather empty without Emma.

The article in the local newspaper mentioning the start of the Arches murder trial only reminded her that she was living on borrowed time.

She pointed out the news story to Galen while he fed Emma her dinner. "How long do you think the trial will run?"

"I don't have any idea," he said. "Several weeks, I'm sure. The wheels of justice grind slowly."

"Then I probably won't have my little house guest for as long as I'd originally thought," she mused aloud.

"It's possible." He paused. "How do you feel about that?"

"I'm happy for Emma and her mother," she said slowly, "but I'll miss her terribly. The apartment will seem so empty without her and her things." She glanced around the room. Baby toys and books lay on the coffee-table and several of Emma's garments were slung over the sofa. Galen had scrounged a baby swing from somewhere and it stood in one corner, next to a play-pen.

"Who am I kidding?" she confessed in a teasing note. "My *life* will seem empty without her. I'll lose my confidante, you know. Emma knows all of my deepest secrets.''

"I'll loan you my ears," he offered.

While it was an attractive proposition, she couldn't possibly accept. Too many of her secret thoughts involved Galen in some way, and the foremost one was why, after their relationship had escalated to a new level these past few weeks, he never talked about the future he'd claimed to want.

She didn't know if it was accidental or intentional. Galen wouldn't say anything he didn't mean, so she didn't have to worry about him making an empty promise, but the reassurance didn't make her stop aching to hear one anyway.

If she didn't stop second-guessing everything, she'd drive herself crazy.

"You can keep your ears," she answered lightly. "Can't have girl-talk with a guy. It's a rule."

"Too bad."

"How do *you* feel about Emma leaving?" she asked.

"You mean, other than the fact that I won't be on call for her fussy moments?" He grinned.

"Hey," she protested, "I only telephoned once at 1:00 a.m. She'd had a rough day. It's not my fault she only wants you when her tummy aches."

"I'm not complaining. I'll take any excuse I can to spend the night."

"If you moved in, you wouldn't need an excuse." She spoke lightly to hide how serious she was.

"No?" His raised eyebrow couldn't have expressed his doubt more eloquently. "You've had two different brothers drop in unexpectedly during the past two weeks. They were startled enough by Emma's presence. How do you think they would have handled the news that I lived here, too?''

Edward and John had both been surprised to see Emma in her apartment. Although they'd accepted her story about the little girl without a second thought, she'd seen the concern in their eyes. Only Edward, as the oldest, had dared to voice the question of how she managed by herself. She'd quickly informed him that if she could be responsible for people whose lives were hanging on by a thread, she could look after one healthy infant.

To her great irritation, Galen had sized up her brothers quite well—probably a guy thing that hearkened back to the days when a man had to mark his territory and know who his enemy was and who his friend. In any case, if they'd known about her new relationship with Galen, they would have grilled her mercilessly about his intentions without a second thought. After struggling to earn her trust, they would ensure that anyone else took the same care with it that they did.

She would have willingly endured every question and been utterly persuasive if she actually *knew* Galen's intentions and could faithfully cling to them.

Oh, he wanted her and had made that quite plain from the beginning. At odd moments, usually when they were in public and nothing could happen, she saw the fire burning in his eyes.

As much as she wanted to hear a vow of commitment, it simply had to come out of his free will rather than her brothers' coercion. Galen might be working to prove his ability to be faithful, but she wondered if he understood that trust and faithfulness only worked on a foundation of love.

''My life is my own,'' she said somewhat loftily.

''But it's still subject to their approval,'' he said. ''I

know you're willing to buck them, but I'm not. I won't be responsible for putting you at odds with your family, so let's leave it at that, shall we?''

She was flattered by his insistence on doing the honorable thing, but during her weaker moments his refusal to move in with her seemed more of a sign that he had reservations about settling down with her than he'd originally claimed.

If she'd been smart, she wouldn't have allowed herself to taste that forbidden and, oh, so addictive fruit without hearing him tell her that he loved her, but she hadn't. They might be friends and now lovers, but she simply had to wait for him to say those magic words.

''Seriously, though,'' he said slowly, as if testing her reaction, ''I think you should consider what you're going to do if Emma's mother doesn't return.''

''Don't you think she will?''

He shrugged. ''We've both seen a lot of sad cases come through the ER. It sounds so dramatic and a little romantic to think Alice was desperate and placed her daughter with someone responsible while she hid from the bad guys, but Emma may not have the happy ending you've pictured. And if she doesn't…''

''Alice has made provisions for her,'' Nikki said, recalling the letter.

''How can you trust a woman you don't know so completely?''

She knew what he was really asking—how could she trust a stranger and not him? Maybe because any hurt that Alice might inflict by not keeping her promise wouldn't come close to what Galen would do to her.

''Woman's intuition. And don't ask me to explain because I can't.''

"And if you're supposed to relinquish her to someone else? Could you do that?"

She'd purposely refused to consider that scenario. She'd hoped that if Alice didn't return, she'd be granted permanent custody. "I'll have to obey her wishes, won't I?"

Suddenly she wondered if Emma's fate had a direct bearing on her own. Before she could ask Galen if he'd mind being an instant father if that should be how things worked out, he pulled the bottle out of Emma's slack-jawed mouth.

"Miss Piglet," he said with his usual affection, "is finished, and just in time. If we leave now, we won't be late for Annie's concert at the fire department."

Her discussion would have to wait. "I hope Emma doesn't scream when she hears the bagpipes."

"Annie's quite good these days." He grinned. "Even Jared, who thought she was being murdered when he first heard her, admits she's come a long way."

"So why hold her concerts at the fire station?"

"They're really not official concerts," he said as Nikki replaced the socks Emma had kicked off. "Annie's a paramedic and bagpipes are often associated with fire departments. The story of her playing for the public is quite involved, so you should ask her for the details."

He rose to place Emma in her carrier and strap her in. "Shall we go?"

Galen drove to Fire Station Number Three, pleasantly surprised to see so many cars parked nearby. "This is quite a crowd," he said as he glanced around the yard and triple driveway where at least two dozen people had placed their folding chairs. Up and down the entire street, people were sitting on their porches or front lawns, clearly waiting for Annie's performance.

Nikki sank onto the stadium chair Galen had unfolded. "Then she doesn't always attract this large a crowd?"

"Not on the occasions I've been here." He noticed Annie standing near the center set of garage doors and watched as Jared maneuvered himself on his crutches to a front-row chair next to the rest of the uniformed firemen. As soon as he was settled, Annie smiled and the music began.

She played for thirty minutes, but to Galen that half-hour passed quickly. He'd set their chairs close together so that he could easily snake his arm around Nikki's shoulders in a casual embrace.

As the music filled the night air, his mind wandered to their earlier conversation. He knew that Nikki wanted him to move in with her and he was more than happy to do so, but his excuse about putting her at odds with her family was only partially correct. The truth of the matter was that he simply felt as if he didn't measure up to her family's high standards. At one time he'd been the sort of fellow they wouldn't have welcomed into the fold, but he was determined to prove his worthiness to Nikki and her strait-laced brothers.

It was quite ridiculous for him to see himself in such an unfavorable light. He was a respected physician now, not the impulsive, footloose high-school and college student he had once been. Yet knowing that his entire future rested on these few weeks was enough to play on any man's insecurities.

But, oh, how he wanted everything she was willing to give. As he traced small circles on her bare arm he felt her shiver, and his masculine pride swelled in his chest. *He* was the one who made Nikki melt and that was a weapon he intended to use every chance he could get.

* * *

Nikki listened to the music, although it was almost impossible to focus while Galen gently stroked her bare arm. His touch had always created an achy awareness inside her, but now it carried a heat that burned hotter and longer than before. She wanted to lean closer to him, to sit so that there wasn't any space between them, but between the chair arms and the crowd around them it was impossible.

Although she didn't recognize any of Annie's tunes, she recognized the song he was playing on her...the song promising a time of making their own beautiful music.

She stole a glance at him and caught him doing the same to her. To the general public he looked quite calm and relaxed, but she saw his heavy-lidded eyes, the barely imperceptible movement of his lips, and the way his throat worked as he swallowed.

Heat began to build inside until she wished Emma would wake up and act as the proverbial cold bucket of water that would force her to yank free of his magnetic pull. As if on cue, the baby ended her nap but, rather than fuss, she sat quietly in her car seat and listened, wide-eyed. Occasionally she waved her hands and threw in rattle music as accompaniment, but otherwise she couldn't have been a more model three-month-old.

After Annie ended her repertoire, the people clapped enthusiastically, a few of the firemen whistled, and the gathering slowly dispersed. Nikki, however, was certain her hair was standing on end from the electricity flowing between Galen and herself. Certain he would see how his presence had affected her and give her that knowing masculine smile he'd perfected, she deliberately avoided his gaze and focused on Annie.

"She was wonderful," Nikki exclaimed. "I never realized how emotional bagpipe music is." Of course, her feelings might have had something to do with the present company, but even if Galen hadn't been with her, her heart would still have been deeply moved.

"You can tell her that in person." Galen guided her through the group until they reached Annie, who had now moved to stand beside Jared.

"You played beautifully," Nikki told her.

Annie laughed. "Oh, I still hit a few wrong notes, but I'm coming along. Right, Jared?" She placed a hand on his shoulder and he grabbed it.

"She's made remarkable progress." He gazed up at her fondly. "Didn't I tell you that you simply needed incentive?"

"He's the one who started this concert thing," she told Nikki. "He'd told the guys that I played the bagpipes, so they dared me to play for them one night. I did."

"And it grew into this." Nikki waved her arms.

"Yeah." Annie's face took on an embarrassed but pleased pink tint. "I sat outside and played, and before I knew it a few of the neighbors came out of their homes and the pedestrians stopped to listen. Next thing I knew, I had more than just my crew for an audience."

"How long have you been playing?"

"My grandfather tried teaching me when I was little, but I wasn't really interested. It wasn't until after he died, and I realized how much I needed this connection to him, that I bought a few books, dredged up what I could remember of his advice from memory, and started."

"You were great," Nikki told her. "Those must have been Scottish songs because I didn't recognize any of them."

"Gaelic," Annie corrected. "The pipes belong to the Gaelic culture and the pieces I chose included 'My Home', 'Highland Laddie', and 'The Road to the Isles'. Those were Grandpa's favorites, so I always include them."

"Your grandfather's teaching must have taken a stronger hold than you think if you can play so well with only books as your instructor."

Annie laughed again. "He probably would be pleased, too. I just tried to remember the things he told me...to relax and blow regularly. And, of course, '*Seinn air a'phiob*', which roughly translates to, 'Sing on the pipes rather than play them.'"

Emma squealed and arched her back as her signal that she was tired of her current view. Nikki hefted her charge onto her shoulder and the baby smiled when she looked in Galen's direction.

"So this is Emma?" A soft look appeared in Annie's eyes. "Galen's told us so much about her. She's quite a charmer."

"She is. And Galen is her buddy. At times he's the only one she wants." Nikki understood completely. She suffered from the same affliction.

"He's a good guy," Annie said simply. "I owe him a lot."

"What do you mean?"

Without warning, the alarm sounded. Like a well-rehearsed drill, people hastily grabbed their chairs off the driveway while the firemen raced to their trucks.

"Gotta run. See you later," Annie called as she hurriedly placed her pipes in a safe place and jumped into the passenger side of the ambulance.

Jared hobbled onto the grass and as Emma began to cry at the noise, Galen took her to cuddle. A few minutes later the trucks pulled out of the station and headed west, their sirens and flashing lights fading into the distance.

"At least Annie got to play her full session," Jared remarked.

"Does this happen often?" Nikki asked.

"About every other week," he admitted cheerfully. "Everyone's learned to expect it...and hope it won't happen the next time. I hear you've been busy, Galen."

Nikki could tell from Jared's expression that he missed being a part of the ER excitement.

"There haven't been any dull moments," Galen answered. "Thank goodness we have Nikki to take up the slack."

Jared nodded. "This is coming off in two weeks," he said, motioning to his ankle cast. "I wanted to come back full time, but Thompson says the most he'll approve is light duty, part time. I think he's going to stick me behind a desk." He finished on a definite sour note.

Nikki realized that she was a little more than halfway through her time in Hope, which also meant that if the Martins didn't return for Emma before then, she would have to take Emma with her. That part didn't bother her, but she knew how Galen doted on the baby and how well the baby had bonded with him. Could she cut those ties for her own convenience?

Or did Galen care? Was she worrying over nothing?

"Don't rush it, buddy," Galen said. "As I said, Nikki is doing well and is a darn sight prettier to look at. Sweeter disposition, too."

Jared chuckled, but something in his eyes made her wonder if he didn't see more than everyone else did.

"Enjoy it while you can," he remarked.

Galen fished his car keys out of his pocket. "Do you need a lift?"

"I'm going to hang around here for a few more hours. Thanks for the offer, though."

As they were driving away, Galen asked, "Do you mind if we stop by my place before I take you home? My landlord is having trouble with the timers on his sprinkler system and he asked me to make sure they shut down tonight. He left town today and won't be back until tomorrow and doesn't want to come back to a waterlogged lawn.''

"Go ahead. We don't mind." Then, because Annie hadn't had time to explain her last comment, Nikki said, "Annie said that she owes you a lot. What did she mean?"

His eyes crinkled with his smile. "I may have played a part in them getting together."

"Matchmaking?" She pretended horror. "I never would have guessed. You definitely have hidden talents."

"It's not like you think," he protested. "Jared and Annie didn't get along at first…she'd forgotten to pay her electric bill but because of an address problem the company cut off his power instead. He thought she needed someone to take her under his wing and he wanted me to do it."

"You? Why you?"

He shrugged one shoulder. "I thought Annie was a special lady and we got along well."

A twinge of jealousy attacked her but, because Annie was a friendly and unassuming individual and didn't act as if she had designs on Galen, Nikki dismissed it.

He continued, "I simply told him that if he was worried about her then he should do it himself."

Seeing the look the two had exchanged, Nikki guessed that, whatever their differences had been, they'd sorted them out. "He obviously did."

"Oh, yeah. They're going to get married. November, I think." He turned a final corner and stopped next to the curb.

His apartment building had been built in the 1970s and showed distinct signs of wear. She was fairly surprised that he hadn't moved into something more suited to his bachelor lifestyle, but she also knew that a doctor couldn't pay off med school loans and live like a king at the same time.

"You can wait for me in my apartment," he said. "It's nothing fancy, but I've heard from a reliable source that my ancient leather recliner is comfy."

"Don't tell me you still have that same old chair," she said, delighted. She'd spent many an hour curled up on it while they'd studied.

His lazy grin reappeared. "OK, I won't say a word. I'll let you be surprised."

After helping her out of the car and unlocking the front door of his ground-floor apartment, he called out a cheery "Make yourself at home" and left.

His living space was infinitely more modern than the apartment he'd rented during their days at St Luke's and, except for the chair he'd dubbed hers, a sturdy, Early American-style sofa and end tables had replaced his vintage garage-sale furniture.

Emma had fallen asleep in her carrier during the short drive, so Nikki placed it on the floor and began walking around Galen's home to see the man he had become.

It was a single bedroom apartment, neat but a little dusty, and his kitchen didn't appear overused. She knew he cooked, but he tended to stick to fast and easy basics, like frying eggs and bacon, grilling a sandwich, or opening a can of soup.

Lately, though, he spent most of his mealtimes with her, so he didn't need much more than the carton of milk, a loaf of bread, a package of lunchmeat, and the beloved Dr Pepper soft drink that she found in his refrigerator.

Returning to the living room, she noticed a bookcase in the corner and she wondered if he was finally indulging his passion for military adventure novels. She found several shelves lined with them, including a few historical works and autobiographies of men who'd changed the course of medicine.

At the bottom she found what looked like an old photo album. Curious, she picked it up, brushed the dust off the cover, and opened it. Inside, she discovered page upon page of photos of Galen as a baby, then a boy, and finally as a college graduate.

Unable to deny herself this unexpected treat, she carried the book to *her* chair and started at the beginning.

Galen had been a beautiful baby, she decided as she saw him grow from infancy to toddlerhood. Just as he aged, the people who posed with him did, too. At first he stood with his mother or father, and then he stood alone, presumably because his mother had taken the pictures after his father had deserted them.

Then he held his little sister. A cute little bundle who had dark hair, big eyes, and a big smile just like…

Emma.

Nikki held her breath as she looked across to compare the baby in the carrier to the baby sleeping in three-year-old Galen's arms.

Other than the clothing, she would have sworn the two were identical.

Her hand shook as she turned the page in search of other pictures. Perhaps it was just a coincidence in the same way that all babies looked remarkably alike.

To her growing dismay, each picture only seemed to hammer home the similarities. This resemblance was not a fluke of the camera, not an aberration of the lens, but something that was evident in photo after photo. Not only did each picture distinctly capture Galen's sister's physical features, but also her lopsided smile, the dimple in her cheek, the way she squinted when laughing.

Exactly the way Nikki saw Emma do now.

Emma's mother was Galen's sister. She had to be.

For her safety, don't tell anyone of her identity. The message Alice Martin had written couldn't have been more plain. If, indeed, she was involved in a high-profile murder trial, Nikki understood about keeping Emma's identity and whereabouts a secret. But to go to such lengths to put Emma in her care, to have *watched* her as the letter had claimed, Alice surely had known that Galen was in town.

Why hadn't she given Emma to *him* for safekeeping, instead of relinquishing her to a total stranger?

Nikki's mind raced with possibilities. Perhaps Emma's identity could be too easily tracked through Galen.

Perhaps Alice was afraid Galen wouldn't want her daughter.

An even more unwelcome thought crossed Nikki's mind. Perhaps, for whatever reason, Alice didn't *want* to involve Galen.

And perhaps Nikki was wrong about everything. Maybe she'd simply contracted a case of Jean's overactive imagination. She hoped so, because she simply couldn't be a party to anything that would hurt Galen.

Determined to prove herself wrong, she doggedly continued through the album. She idly noticed his transformation from a boy to a teenager but diligently watched for pictures of his sister. By the time Nikki studied the last snapshots of his sister, she couldn't deny the facts any longer.

The Alice Martin she'd met in her office was simply an older, more time-worn version of the teenage girl who so clearly had adored her older brother.

Questions pounded her like hailstones. Should she tell Galen her suspicions? Should she wait and hope that Alice would make contact with Galen?

And if Alice didn't, could Nikki live with herself, knowing that she had information to set his mind at ease about his sibling's whereabouts and hadn't shared it?

The door opened and he breezed in. ''All done,'' he said cheerfully.

Nikki snapped the album closed and forced her expression into relaxed lines. ''Any problems?'' she asked.

''A few, which is why it took longer than I'd expected, but the water won't be running all night.'' He looked at her. ''What have you been doing?''

Now wasn't the time for him to look through the pictures with her. If he saw the resemblance between his sister's baby pictures and Emma, she'd have to tell him what she knew or suspected. Until she'd thoroughly thought this situation through, Galen's trip down memory lane would have to wait.

''Just looking through your photo album,'' she said, hastily rising to replace it on the shelf. ''I hope you don't mind.''

He shrugged. ''Not at all. It's been a long time since I looked through it myself.''

''I could tell from the dust. Your mom took a lot of pictures of you.''

He smiled. ''I understand it's part of the first-kid-and-everything-he-does-is-cute syndrome.''

''My brothers complained about the same thing. Edward has tons of snapshots and Derek doesn't have very many.''

''What about you? You came after Derek.''

''Ah, but I was the first girl, so that put me in the same league as Edward in the picture-taking department.''

''You'll have to show them to me some time.''

''They're at my place in Blue Springs,'' she said, ''but, yeah, I will. I saw some of your sister, too. What was her name again?''

''Mary.''

Mary. Maybe she'd changed her name to avoid being traced, but did that mean the legal papers weren't legal? Nikki's mind raced with possibilities, then decided that if Alice—er, Mary—had involved a lawyer, then there couldn't have been any shady dealings, could there?

Although she wanted to ask more questions, she didn't dare out of fear of raising Galen's suspicions. Deciding to put as much distance as possible between herself and the album, she asked brightly, "Shall we go? It's almost time for Emma's bath."

"All right." He picked up her carrier and smiled at her sleeping form. "I know this sounds crazy, but she's got to be the prettiest baby I've ever seen."

"You're prejudiced because you're around her so much."

"I guess. Still, there's something about her that reminds me of someone…"

Nikki didn't let him finish his sentence. "You know what they say, everyone has a twin somewhere in the world. I wouldn't dwell on it, if I were you."

She made a beeline to the door, determined to avoid the subject of babies and resemblances. Before she touched on this topic again, she wanted to weigh her choices and consider all the consequences.

Galen followed her out and locked the door behind him. "As much sleep as Emma has gotten today, I hope she sleeps tonight."

Nikki nodded her agreement, although in truth it didn't matter if Emma was awake or quietly dreaming her baby dreams. With these new facts staring her in the face, Nikki wouldn't sleep at all.

CHAPTER NINE

GALEN strode toward the MEC the next morning, eager to see if Nikki's preoccupation from last night had faded. He'd first noticed it after Annie's bagpipe concert and wondered if Jared's mention of coming back to work in a couple of weeks had caught her by surprise, too.

Had a month gone by already? It didn't seem like it—a few days, a week at the most. However long the time, it had been four weeks of simply reconnecting with Nikki.

What about those nights when you two set the sheets on fire? his conscience asked. *That sounds a little stronger than simply* reconnecting.

An involuntary sheepish grin crossed his face. OK, so they'd done more than just renew their former acquaintance. The speed at which they'd jumped to an intimate relationship only proved what he'd suspected all along…Nikki was the woman who suited him as if they'd been made for each other. She was the one who made him realize that he wasn't like his father, that he could have what everyone else took for granted. She was the one he wanted, not just for today but for *every* day.

She was the one he loved.

The question was, did she feel the same?

Up until now they'd concentrated on the present and hadn't touched on the proverbial tomorrow. In his opinion it hadn't been necessary. He'd stated his intentions from the beginning and had wanted to let their relationship develop without pressuring her. He'd been operating under the belief that he'd hit the ball in her court and she had to make the next move, but Jared had inadvertently reminded him how quickly they were approaching the end of the current game.

He'd thought about discussing the issue of where they went from here after Nikki had tucked Emma into bed last night, but she'd seemed so distant that he'd decided to wait. On the heels of that thought came another that raised all sorts of warning flags.

She was acting exactly as she had during their final weeks of residency, when she'd closed herself off and pretended that everything had been fine when it hadn't been.

As far as he was concerned, that didn't bode well for him. Rather than discussing their options, she'd been jumpy and uncommunicative, which only indicated that she either dreaded making a decision or, worse yet, she dreaded *telling* him of her decision. The timing was just too coincidental to be otherwise.

He might fearlessly wade into an emergency situation, deal with Code Blues and handle a man's internal organs without batting an eyelash, but when it came to this, when it came to risking personal disappointment, he was as hesitant as a first-year medical student.

He could have pushed forward anyway, but he wasn't any more eager to hear bad news than Nikki obviously was to give it. The problem was, both of them had abandonment issues to work out and both of them had trouble talking about their innermost thoughts. They'd shared more of themselves when they'd been residents, but that was what friends did. When they'd made the leap to lovers, the rules had subtly changed. The future had become a forbidden topic, as if they both expected to hurt each other and were trying to protect themselves from it.

Maybe he should have told her that he'd dropped a few strongly worded hints in Dr Thompson's ears about adding another physician to their ER service. Knowing that she would be employed if she remained at Hope might make the difference.

Knowing that he loved her might sway her decision, too. Then again, it might not.

If only he could get her to talk, to open up and tell him what was on her mind. He couldn't counter her arguments if he didn't know what they were.

Knowing he'd find Nikki in her office this early, he stopped there first. She was sitting in her chair, staring out the window, looking as neat as always but extremely exhausted.

"Did Emma keep you awake?" he commiserated.

She swiveled in her chair and gave him a weak smile before she began to flip through a chart on her desk. "Yeah. I gave Susan strict orders to keep her from napping all day. As noisy as the little people crowd was when I dropped Em off, she shouldn't have any trouble."

He'd noticed that she avoided his gaze, just as she had last night. "Wound up, were they?"

She nodded. "Susan said it means the weather will change."

"Really? I wonder if her prediction will be more accurate than the meteorologists'."

"Who knows? But it sounds good to me." She hid a yawn behind her hand.

"You need some coffee."

"I'm on my way to get a cup."

"The stuff in the ER pot is stronger."

"If Jean's brew doesn't do the trick, I'll be over to beg some."

His pager beeped. Duty called, so he quickly addressed the question he'd come to ask. "See you for lunch? Or would you rather take a nap?"

"Right now I'd vote for a nap," she said ruefully, "but I'll keep my options open."

"Since you mentioned options," he began, "we should talk about what we'll do after Jared returns."

She froze. "We should," she said slowly, "but we can wait a few weeks, can't we? We don't need to make any decisions today."

"No, but we shouldn't wait until the last minute either."

"I understand, but we also have Emma to consider." Her laugh sounded forced. "I just realized...we have enough variables coming into play that our lives seem like a complicated algebraic equation."

"It's not that complicated to me. You either want to stay here in Hope with me, or you don't."

"I do, but..." She rubbed her forehead as if to ease a headache.

"But what?"

"But I have so many things to sort out. Emma is one of them. I can't make any sort of decision unless I know if she will or won't fit into our lives."

"Becoming an instant father won't bother me."

Her smile was tight. "I didn't think it would."

"Then what's the problem?"

"I just need a few more weeks," she begged. "Please?"

What choice did he have? Galen nodded slowly. If she didn't want to talk right now, if she had to sort through things in her own mind before she did, then he'd be patient for the next two weeks. Maybe by then they'd have a clearer picture of what lay ahead for all of them.

On Wednesday evening, Emma decided that no one but Galen could make her happy, so while he tucked her into bed Nikki retreated to the thinking spot on her balcony. The night air was still warm but it was quiet except for the chirp of the crickets and the occasional door slam. The stars blinked into existence one by one and out of habit she located the North Star via the Big Dipper. It may have helped early sailors find their way on the high seas, but unfortunately, it wasn't doing much to help her set the course of her life.

She'd debated what to do with her suspicions about Emma for almost three days and had finally reached her decision. She simply didn't have the heart to tell Galen, because she couldn't stand knowing that she would be the one who put the hurt in his eyes.

She loved him too much to do that.

He might pretend that the news didn't bother him, but she knew it would. Who wouldn't be crushed by the knowledge that one's own sister wouldn't contact him or seek him out when she was in trouble? That she'd prefer to rely on a total stranger than a blood relative? How could she not trust her own brother?

No, it was Alice's responsibility to contact him and to explain, not hers.

And yet how could she expect Alice/Mary to trust Galen when she didn't?

It's not that she didn't trust him, she defended herself. She'd seen the women he preferred—tall, leggy blondes who had perfected the art of being coy—women like Susan.

Nikki had stopped at the day-care center during her late lunch-break and she'd seen the two of them chatting away moments before Susan had stepped close and hugged him. She'd tried to tell herself that it was all very innocent and not very mature on her part to go into orbit every time a female under the age of sixty-five spoke to him, but it was little things like this that only activated her insecurities. She just didn't know how to stop this fruitless agonizing.

Maybe if she fit the description of the Susans, the Trinas, and the Annabelles, she wouldn't worry so much, but the fact was, she didn't. For all she knew, she was simply a novelty that would someday wear off.

She sensed Galen's presence before he joined her at the railing. "She's asleep," he said. "Finally."

Nikki grinned. "Have you noticed that when she's extra tired, she wants you?"

"Yeah. I can't figure out why, though."

Nikki wondered if Emma sensed her blood tie with Galen on some elemental level. "Maybe she just goes for the strong, silent type."

"Probably," he agreed. "Speaking of silent types, you've been quiet the last few days."

She decided to bluff. "Have I?"

"Yeah. Any particular reason?"

"I've had a lot on my mind, I suppose."

"Like what?"

Nikki glanced at him, seeing his face wreathed in a shadow cast by the light shining behind him.

"I called my boss today," she said.

"And?"

"I asked for a month's vacation after I finish my contract at Hope."

"Really? You didn't have another job waiting?"

"I refused to go for personal reasons."

He leaned his left side against the railing in a picture of ease that contrasted sharply with his intent gaze. "Where are you planning to spend your vacation?"

"Why, here, of course."

His face relaxed into a smile. "What made you decide to stick around town?"

She had several reasons, none of which she could explain. While it was true that she couldn't bear the thought of leaving him behind, she still had her doubts about them staying a couple for the long haul. Granted, ninety per cent of her believed they could make it work, but the remaining ten per cent was enough to make her hesitate.

Then there was the matter of Emma. If these weeks were Galen's only opportunity to spend time with his niece, then she wanted them to last as long as possible. It would be her gift to him, although he would never know it.

"It seemed silly to uproot Emma for a few weeks," she said instead.

"Good idea, but what would you have decided if Emma hadn't been a consideration?"

"But she was, so it doesn't matter, does it?" she prevaricated.

"I suppose not," he answered slowly.

But somehow Nikki received the impression that it did.

On Thursday afternoon, Nikki scolded herself for falling back into her old habits of hugging her feelings to herself. She could fight other people's battles without batting an eye and wade into someone else's fray without hesitation, yet when it came time to fight for herself she either gave up at the first sign of resistance or let someone else take the initiative.

She should have told Galen how she'd felt last night, instead of dancing around the issue or waiting for him to pledge his undying love. So why hadn't she?

On Friday, before she could puzzle out the answer to her own question, which was still niggling at her, her pager beeped. She called the ER, learned that they were expecting several car accident victims and could she be there in ten minutes?

She arrived in five and had started to gown up in the

disposable protective gown, latex gloves, and face shield when Galen joined her.

"MVAs are starting early," he remarked as he slipped the yellow gown over his royal blue scrub suit.

"It's Friday," she said. "Everyone gets in a rush because they're going out of town for the weekend."

"Probably headed to the lake. It's where people go to beat the heat."

"Not me," she teased. "I can't swim."

"You can't? Why not?"

"It's not that I can't swim," she corrected. "I can, a little, but I have to be able to see and touch the bottom. Who knows what dangerous sea creatures lurk beneath the surface?"

He laughed. "Sea creatures, eh? I doubt if any relatives of the Loch Ness monster live in the lake around here."

"One never knows." Then, becoming more serious, she asked, "What are we expecting?"

"The usual. Spinal injuries, internal bleeding, the whole nine yards."

"How many?"

"Four. Three males and one female. According to the paramedics' report, the male and female in the compact car are in worse shape than the two guys in the pickup."

"Is Radiology ready?" she asked.

"And waiting. Lab and respiratory therapy are on their way."

Ravi yelled from the ambulance bay door, "They're here."

Galen pulled on his face shield and a pair of latex gloves. "It's show time."

Nikki waited for the paramedics to bring in the victims. Annie and her partner had their hands full with the male and female while their two colleagues were busy with the two men they had transported.

Galen waved Nikki into the trauma room with the two men and she rapidly assessed the twenty-two-year-old driver who was deemed to have the more severe injuries. He was strapped to his backboard and complained of chest pain. Because his breathing was labored, she immediately ordered a chest and sinus X-ray after deciding that the blood covering his face was from a broken nose.

His passenger, who appeared to be the same age, had suffered bumps, bruises, and facial lacerations, which would also require stitches. Otherwise he was fine, and the lab results confirmed it later.

"Will I have scars all over my face?" he asked.

"Not if I do my job right," she answered with a smile.

His buddy, who'd just returned from Radiology and was lying in the next bed, managed a chuckle. "You were too pretty anyway, Todd."

"Speak for yourself, AJ," Todd told him. "At least I won't end up with a buzzard beak."

"You're just jealous. Big noses are a sign of virility, aren't they, Doc?" AJ asked.

"Sorry, but I don't recall hearing that in medical school," she returned.

"Maybe someone should do a study," AJ said.

Nikki carefully sutured Todd's face while the two men bantered back and forth in an obvious attempt to release the stress of knowing they could just as easily have landed in the morgue as the emergency room. Nikki reviewed AJ's X-rays, cleared him from the immobilizing backboard and collar and instructed him not to lift anything and to rest until the hairline fractures in his lower ribs healed.

"Aren't you going to tape them?" he asked, sounding nasal because of the packing in his nose.

"We don't do that any more. Just rest, use ice and heat intermittently for the next twenty-four hours, and if you hurt too bad, take your usual pain medication. If you have any problems, come back."

"And my nose?" He lifted the ice pack.

"That's next." She straightened the crooked part with a sharp jerk and surveyed her handiwork while he yelled, "Ow."

"That wasn't so bad, was it?"

"Speak for yourself," he grumbled, gingerly touching the offended part of his face.

"It's aligned again, but don't be surprised if you see a little bump or two when the swelling goes down," she said as she splinted it with tape.

After giving him a prescription for an antibiotic and learning that his tetanus immunization was current, she released both men into the care of their waiting relatives.

She left the room and headed for the nurses' station, but before she reached it Galen motioned to her from the doorway of his trauma room.

"I need you," he mouthed.

She switched directions. "What's up?"

"The woman. A girl, actually. Sixteen. Her injuries aren't consistent with being bounced around in a car."

"What are you saying?"

"Her boyfriend used her as a punch bag," he said bluntly.

"Some boyfriend. Was she sexually assaulted?"

"Not that she'll admit to. I thought maybe she'd rather talk to another woman so would you mind?"

She nodded. Taking the chart out of Galen's hand, she strode into the trauma room, glad to see that the girl's partner had been assigned to another cubicle. "Hi,

Melanie,'' she said with a warm smile. "I'm Dr
Lawrence.''

Melanie sniffled, but didn't answer. She was a blonde,
with short, spiky hair and thick mascara-lined eyes. A
pretty girl, if not for the red, puffy mark on her left cheek.
Several bruises in varying shades of purple to blue-green
were evident above the neckline of her patient gown and
she cradled her newly plastered left arm in its sling.

A clean break of the radius, according to the attached
copy of the radiology report.

"You've been banged up pretty good,'' Nikki said off-
handedly. "It's understandable since you just survived a
serious accident.''

"Yeah,'' came the sullen reply.

"Dr Stafford tells me, though, that not all of your injuries are from the car wreck.''

"So?'' Melanie's defiance was obvious in her one word,
but Nikki looked past her bravado to the scared teenager
underneath.

Nikki exchanged a quick glance with Galen, who tipped
his head slightly as if to say that he'd seen it, too. "If the
guy who was with you is responsible—''

"It's none of your business.''

"I'm a doctor and you're in our hospital. Of course it's
our business,'' Nikki said, keeping her tone low and non-
threatening.

"He said—'' Melanie glared past Nikki's shoulder at
Galen "—I only had a broken arm. It's fixed and now I
want to go.''

"If your boyfriend—''

"He's *not* my boyfriend.''

"Then who is he?''

Melanie shrugged. "I met Billy Joe a week ago. I
needed a ride and he gave me one.''

"He also gave you those bruises, didn't he?"

Melanie looked away and didn't answer.

Nikki exchanged another glance with Galen and he simply raised both eyebrows. "Did he do anything else to you?" she asked. "Anything like—"

"We didn't have sex if that's what you're asking," Melanie snapped. "He wanted to, but…" Her voice faded as she bit her already swollen lip.

"But you didn't," Nikki finished gently. "Is that why he hit you?"

Melanie didn't move, then finally nodded once.

Nikki had seen this scenario a hundred times. "We should call your parents."

"No." Melanie nearly bolted out of bed. "You can't call them."

"Why not?"

"Because…"

Galen stepped closer to the bed. "You're not injured enough to be admitted and Billy Joe is. He'll be here for several days at least. Where will you go?"

Her hazel eyes darted back and forth. "Somewhere."

"Where are you from?"

A familiar mulish expression crossed her face. "It doesn't matter. Can I have my clothes back now?"

Without a medical reason they couldn't keep her, but Nikki refused to be responsible for turning a sixteen-year-old onto the streets. She started to protest, but Galen answered Melanie's question.

"They're in the bag on the shelf underneath your bed. Holler if you need help. I'll send a nurse in."

Nikki followed him out of the cubicle. "We can't just let her walk out of here."

"I know."

"She has no place to go."

"I know."

"What if she winds up with someone worse than Billy Joe?"

"Nikki," he said impatiently, "I *know*. This isn't my first day on the job."

Nikki calmed down. "Then what are we going to do?"

He ran his fingers through his hair, obviously as frustrated as she was. Melanie's situation had probably hit him quite hard because of his personal experience.

"First," he began slowly, "we're going to talk her into calling her parents. If that won't work, we'll have to bring in the police. She's a runaway and a minor, so we have no choice."

"And how do you propose to convince her to contact her family?"

Determination darkened his already dark eyes. "I'm not sure, but somehow I will. Just follow my lead. OK?"

"Whatever you say."

As soon as Melanie was decent, Nikki accompanied Galen into the room. This time she hovered near the foot of the bed to observe and play whatever role Galen had planned while he approached the girl.

"I just need to check your vital signs once more before you leave," he said as he placed his fingers on her wrist to take her pulse. Then he added casually, "From your accent, I'd say you grew up in the South. Georgia?"

Melanie looked taken aback, as if surprised he'd guessed correctly, then turned her head to stare into the corner. "You're guessing."

"You're a long way from home," he remarked.

"I told you. I caught a ride."

"Have you eaten today?"

Melanie frowned. "N-no."

"Then I hope you'll stay long enough to eat in our cafeteria before you go." He grinned. "My treat."

She looked suspicious. "Why are you being so nice?"

"Because I'm a nice person," he answered promptly. "Just ask me."

A glimmer of a smile tugged at her mouth.

"I bet you don't get regular meals, do you?"

"Not usually. But it's OK. I'm not starving or anything. Not like the kids in Africa."

"True. Since you mentioned kids, do you have any brothers or sisters?" He moved on to listen to her heart and Nikki noticed that he took his sweet time, just as he had when taking Melanie's pulse. At first she didn't understand why, but as the conversation continued, she silently applauded him for his tactics.

"A little sister."

"Do you miss her?"

Melanie paused. "Yeah. We were buddies."

"How long have you been gone?"

"A month."

"I see. You know, my sister ran away from home when she was your age," he said idly. "To this day I've never seen or heard from her. We were buddies, too."

Melanie's interest was roused and her confidence seemed to waver. "Never?"

"Never," he said firmly. "My mother cried and I couldn't eat for days because we couldn't understand why she left. Then we worried that something had happened, that she had died and we'd never be able to fix whatever had caused her to leave in the first place. I prayed every night that she'd come back, or at least telephone."

"Maybe…maybe she didn't think she could," she said in a small voice.

"Then she thought wrong," he said firmly. "There was

nothing she could have done that would have made us willingly let her go. I'll bet your family feels the same way about you.''

She studied her fingernails. "Maybe."

"Then again, if you don't care that they're suffering, then it doesn't matter, does it? Maybe it doesn't bother you to know that you're probably making your little sister cry, your mom worry, and no one able to sleep at night.''

"I care." She tossed her head defiantly. "But my dad is pretty tough. I can't do *anything* without his permission. He watched me like a hawk all the time.''

Nikki hoped the girl meant that in the strict sense of a parent's concerned eye rather than any sexual interest. Child abuse took many forms and she hoped Melanie hadn't left home because of it.

Galen obviously thought the same thing because he asked, "Did he ever hurt you or touch you in an inappropriate way?"

"No. Nothing like that. He was just crazy about all of his rules. 'Don't do this, Melanie,' she mimicked. "'Don't do that, Melanie.' 'So-and-so isn't a good influence. He or she doesn't have a good reputation.' I felt so...so *stifled*. Like I couldn't breathe or think for myself.''

Nikki felt herself relax. Thank goodness they didn't have to worry about a man taking indecent liberties with his own daughter.

"Maybe he was only trying to protect you. To keep you safe," Galen said. "Fathers do that, you know.''

"He was always wanting to know who my friends were and what we were doing," she blurted out. "I didn't have any privacy at all!''

"I'm not saying he handled things in the right way," he commented as he reattached the blood-pressure cuff to her arm and pumped it up, "but give him credit for caring what happened to you. The world can be a scary place but, after being on your own, you've seen that for yourself.''

She frowned, then nodded.

''I'm sure you've also learned the importance of choosing your friends wisely,'' Galen continued. ''Unless, of course, you don't mind having a guy beat you up until you give him what he wants.''

Once again Melanie chewed on her lower lip. ''What if my folks don't want me to come back? They're probably so ashamed…''

''They're frantic with worry,'' he said, ''but you won't know what they feel unless you call.''

''I don't know what to say.''

''Start by telling them you're OK. I have a suspicion you won't have to say anything else.''

Again Melanie hesitated, as if her yearning to go home and the fear associated with doing so warred within her.

''I tell you what,'' he said, unwrapping the cuff and stowing it in the wall holder above the bed. ''If you want me to, I can talk to your parents first and get an idea of the situation. Then if they're not receptive to the idea of you coming home, I'll hang up and you won't have to say a word.''

The relief on her face made the haggard lines disappear. ''Could you? You'd do that for me?''

He reached for the telephone. ''Give me the number and I'll dial right now.''

He cast a sidelong glance at Nikki, flashed a triumphant smile, then punched in the number that Melanie recited. Feeling extraneous and utterly drained from the emotional experience, Nikki left the room.

Galen had always glossed over the situation with his sister with the most minor of details. Now, after hearing his perspective and realizing the pain he suffered over not knowing her fate, Nikki's decision to keep her information about Emma to herself bordered on cruelty. How inhuman would she be to let him form a special bond with his niece and never tell him her true identity?

She simply had to divulge what she knew…or what she *thought* she knew. When Alice/Mary returned, Nikki would be as eloquent as Galen had been with Melanie. By the time she finished, Alice/Mary wouldn't be able to walk away, no matter what she'd originally intended.

Of course, Nikki had the added leverage of holding her daughter. She simply wouldn't hand Emma over until she could give Galen part of the family he'd lost so many years ago.

CHAPTER TEN

NIKKI waited outside for several minutes, intending to corner Galen as soon as he finished with Melanie. However, her pager went off and she scurried back to the MEC after leaving word that she wanted to see Galen as soon as he was free.

"What's the emergency?" she asked Jean.

"The phone." Jean held out the receiver. "Your brother."

Her heart skipped a beat. Had something happened? "I'll take it in my office."

A minute later, Derek's familiar voice drifted over the wire. "Hi, sis."

"Hi to you, too. What's the big emergency? Is everything all right?"

"Yeah. I just have a conference call scheduled in ten minutes and I wanted to be sure to get through to you before then."

"Derek!" she yelled in his ear. "I think my work is a little more important than discussing someone's order for baseball bats and athletic supporters."

"Now, sis. Calm down."

"I am calm. I was worried, dammit. Don't you ever scare me like that again."

"Sorry," he said, clearly unrepentant. "So how are things going in Hope?"

"OK. I'm going to take my month's vacation here."

"No kidding? Lots to see and do in Hope, is there?"

"Enough to keep me busy."

"How's Galen?"

"Fine," she answered warily. "Why do you ask?"

"Just making conversation, Nik."

"Hey, Derek," she began, wanting to ask his opinion and wondering if she truly wanted to hear it, "can I ask you a question?"

"Shoot."

"Why did I let you guys always fight my battles?"

He sounded curious. "What brought this up?"

"Just answer the question."

He chuckled. "Because we were bigger than you."

"Seriously."

"Because you were cute."

She ignored his comment. "Was I that helpless?"

This time it took him a few seconds to answer. "You weren't helpless as much as defeated."

"Defeated?"

"Yeah. You acted as if you didn't deserve to have the things the rest of us took for granted."

Could that be why she still struggled to fight for what she wanted? Because deep down she thought she didn't deserve them?

"Oh."

"Since you're asking, do I need to round up the rest of our knightly brothers to fight whatever dragon is troubling our fair lady?"

She laughed at his fake courtly words. "No, thanks. It was just a rhetorical question."

"Well, then, if you don't have any dragons to slay, I'll let you go. My call is about to go through."

As she hung up the phone, she hoped she'd convinced him not to assemble the family and descend upon her *en masse*, because the dragons she faced now were ones she had to slay for herself.

Determined to tackle the first and most immediate one, she returned to the ER and found Galen at the nurses' station, talking on the phone.

"How did it go with Melanie's parents?" she asked as soon as he replaced the receiver.

He leaned back in the chair, folded his arms across his chest and grinned from ear to ear. "They're on their way."

"I'm so glad. For all of them."

He nodded. "Me, too."

"If you're ready for lunch, I'd really like to talk to you," she began.

His expression turned apologetic. "I hate to renege, but I promised Melanie that I'd feed her. Fern scrounged up a sandwich for her and she ate so fast I thought she'd inhale the Cellophane wrapper, too."

She couldn't very well tell him to let the teenager go without food. "That's OK. I understand."

"Thanks." His gaze grew intent. "Is this something important or can it wait?"

Now that Nikki had made up her mind to tell him about Emma and Alice, she didn't want another delay, but in the grand scheme of things, what would a few more hours hurt?

"It can wait." She smiled to set his mind at ease. "If you have time this afternoon, drop by my office."

"Will do."

With that out of the way, at least temporarily, her thoughts returned to Melanie. "So her parents were really excited to hear from her?"

"Elated."

"And how's Melanie? Other than being hungry."

"The kid looks ten years younger. Their family troubles aren't over, but maybe this episode will convince them to see a counselor."

"I'll bet her parents are ready to kiss your feet," she teased.

His eyes gleamed with an unholy light. "I can think of more pleasurable body parts to kiss."

Her face warmed under his heated gaze. "So can I," she whispered.

With Galen occupied for lunch, Nikki spent her hour with Emma in the day-care center. Afterwards she had a full afternoon of patients, but her busy schedule didn't stop her from watching for Galen's arrival.

At four o'clock, just as her day started to wind down at long last, Jean caught her in the hallway, grabbed her arm and hauled her into their medication room.

"You aren't going to believe this," she said, her voice squeaky from excitement.

"Calm down," Nikki advised. "You're going to have a heart attack."

Jean drew a deep breath. "You're right. You're still not going to believe this."

"Someone from *America's Most Wanted* is in our waiting room?"

She sniffed. "Joke all you want, but you're going to croak when you hear."

"When I hear what?"

"Mrs Martin is back."

A sickening feeling attacked Nikki's stomach. "Are you sure?"

"Of course I'm sure. She wants to see you."

Wondering what had prompted this new development when she didn't think the trial had ended, Nikki squared her shoulders. "What about the rest of the patients?"

"We have a fellow with a rash, but he's the last unless someone else walks in."

"I'll see him before I talk to Mrs Martin," Nikki decided. "She can wait in my office in the meantime."

Nikki immediately diagnosed Gary Carter's problem as a case of contact dermatitis from the poison ivy he'd been clearing out of his field. She quickly dispensed a corticosteroid ointment, along with detailed instructions ranging from washing his clothes separately from the rest of his family's to using calamine lotion for the itching, then sent him on his way.

Before she opened the door to her office, she drew a bracing breath and hoped this was only a whirlwind check-on-Emma visit because she wasn't mentally prepared to become childless at a moment's notice. By the same token, she hoped Galen would be busy for a little longer.

She went inside to find Alice pacing in her high heels and looking like an executive in her short blue skirt and white blouse. Even with age and her fine clothes, she still resembled the girl in Galen's photo album.

"Hi, Alice," Nikki said, closing the door behind her. "Or should I say Mary?"

Mary's jaw dropped. "You know?"

"I guessed," Nikki said as she moved to sit behind her desk. "I wasn't expecting you for several more weeks. Has the trial ended already?"

This time Mary gasped. "You know about that, too?"

"I guessed," she repeated. "Actually, it was a fluke. Galen and I'd been watching the news and a picture of the Arches courtroom flashed on. I recognized you. Or I thought it was you."

"Then Galen knows?"

Nikki shook her head. "He knows that Alice Martin left her baby with me because she was somehow involved in the Arches trial, but I didn't tell him that I thought you were his sister."

Mary heaved a sigh. "I don't know if I should thank you or wish that you had."

"You have to see him," Nikki insisted. "To tell him you're alive and that the little girl he loves is his niece. You will, won't you? By the way, what *is* your name?"

"Alice is a family name that's been passed down through the family from my great-grandmother." Her smile became rueful. "Apparently having several Alices was rather confusing, so the rest of the family starting referring to them by their middle names. By the time I came along, no one bothered to call me anything but Mary."

No wonder Galen hadn't been remotely suspicious. Mary was a common enough name that he wouldn't possibly make any connection.

"I was going to tell Galen today about you and Emma," Nikki began. "I hadn't planned to at first, but then I realized that he needs to know the truth."

Suddenly Galen stood framed in the doorway, his face grim. "What do I need to know?"

Galen saw Nikki's guilty expression and wondered what was going on until he saw her glance at the woman in the armchair. He shifted his gaze to her and finally saw a sight that left him reeling in shock.

She rose. "Hello, Galen."

"Mary?" he asked hoarsely.

Her smile trembled as she nodded. "It's me."

Words failed him. He stood, stunned, staring at the woman who was an older version of the girl he remembered. She took a step forward, and the next thing he knew he was hugging her and fighting back the lump of emotion in his throat.

"You came back," he breathed. "After all this time, I never thought I'd see you again."

"Me, too."

"How did you find me?"

She stiffened and drew back. "It's a long story."

"Mary is our mysterious Alice Martin," Nikki announced in the background.

He looked at Mary, then at Nikki, and back at his sister. "Then that means…"

"Emma is your niece," Mary finished.

He shook his head, scarcely able to sort through this tangled web. "I don't understand."

"I told you it's a long story," Mary reminded him.

"I'm not going anywhere." He pulled up another chair and sat down. After all this time he didn't intend to let Mary out of his sight because he might blink and discover that he'd imagined the entire thing.

Mary took her seat again and folded her hands in her lap. "I'm not sure where to start."

"The beginning is a good place," he said wryly.

"After I left home—"

"Why *did* you leave?" he interrupted.

"I was young and stupid and believed the wrong guy," she said flatly. "Jim wanted to go to California to start over."

Jim? "James Bowman? You were hanging around with him?" Galen was aghast. "He was one step away from prison."

"Galen," Nikki chided. "Let her tell her story."

Mary's grateful glance at Nikki didn't escape Galen's notice and he clamped his mouth closed.

"Anyway," Mary continued, "I soon realized that Jim couldn't start over because he made his own troubles. By the time I learned that, I'd made so many bad decisions idn't know how to straighten myself out. He left and I ved hand to mouth for a while, doing odd jobs. Eventually I was hired as a waitress at a truck stop. The wner took me under her wing and encouraged me to finsh high school.''

''Why didn't you ever call?'' he demanded.

''You were the smart one of the family,'' she said simly. ''Everyone always compared me to you, especially Mom, and I came up short. So I thought I'd wait until I'd nade something of myself. Eventually, I'd found out Mom ad died and heard you were in med school. By then I vanted you to be proud of me, so I enrolled in classes at he community college and found a job as a secretary.''

''Where does Emma come into it?''

''When I went to work for Mr Arches, I met a man who lso worked for him—Henry Lucas. We started seeing ach other, and talked about getting married once we knew Emma was on the way. But Henry had some concerns bout the way Mr Arches did business and we both suspected that he was involved in something shady. A few nonths later Henry's car went over an embankment and e was killed. The police said someone had tampered with is brakes and I knew his death wasn't an accident.''

Nikki broke in. ''Who was the older man I saw you vith in the courtroom?''

''Henry's father. He insisted on being there. Anyway, I vas afraid so I contacted the police and told them everyning I knew about Arches's accounting practices and busiess deals. For my safety and Emma's, I started using the ame of Martin.''

''And you came to Hope.''

She nodded. ''The district attorney decided that it would e safer for Emma if she and I weren't in the same place vhile we waited for the case to go to trial. I hated to leave her, but Mr Arches has rather long arms,'' she added ruefully. "So I thought of you. Most people didn't know [I] even had a brother, which was exactly the type of person I needed. After the DA found you, I came to Hope, intending to beg you to take care of Emma.''

"But you didn't leave Emma with me," he said, as the cold spot in his chest grew. "Did you?"

She squirmed in her chair. "I was going to, but the more I thought about it, the more I didn't know how you'd react to having your long-lost sister show up and ask you to look after a baby. I was ready to take my chances when I realized that if the DA had found you without any trouble, Arches's henchmen could, too. Emma's safety was my main concern, so when I was hanging around the hospital trying to decide what to do, Nikki seemed like my perfect answer. I'd planned to come to you when everything was over and explain. Honest.''

"That doesn't justify why you couldn't have shared your plan with me beforehand. I would have understood your reasons.''

She avoided his gaze, and he knew there was something else she hadn't told him. He cast around, trying to imagine what it might have been. "Did you think I wouldn't want Emma? Or that I would brag to the world that she was my niece when I knew the importance of secrecy? Didn't you *trust* me?"

His question hung in the air like thick fog.

Mary pursed her lips, then finally answered. "I was also afraid you might do something so I couldn't get Emma back.''

"Not give her back?" he said incredulously, ignoring Nikki's gasp across the room.

"You were always complaining about how irresponsible Dad was for leaving us, and after I ran away with Jim, knew you'd think the same thing about me. You'd turned into a responsible doctor while I was a struggling secretary, which only made me feel even more insecure. I was scared that you'd use my youthful indiscretions against me and try to get custody of Emma on the grounds that I was an unfit mother. Putting Emma in Dr Lawrence's care and keeping my identity a secret seemed the lesser of two potential evils.''

From where he sat, his sister had put her faith in a stranger rather than in him because he'd become a potential evil. The sister whom he'd adored, the sister he'd looked after, had thought he was so mean-spirited that he'd take away something so precious to her. If his own flesh and blood didn't consider him worthy of trust, then how could he possibly expect any other woman to do what she could not? The ache in his chest grew stronger.

"I'm sorry," Mary said faintly. "I was wrong to think the worst of you. I know that now, but I was only trying to prepare for every eventuality, to protect the little piece of Henry that I still had. Can you forgive me?''

He rubbed the bridge of his nose, trying to sort through her revelations and his fragile emotions. At the moment, too many internal wounds were bleeding for him to feel magnanimous and grant her the forgiveness she sought.

He focused on Nikki. "Were you in on her deception?''

"No!'' Nikki shook her head. "I didn't figure it out until the day we visited your apartment. The evening I looked at your photo album.''

No wonder she'd been preoccupied. She'd been hiding the truth from him when she should have mentioned her suspicions.

The V-neckline of his scrub top suddenly seemed too tight. He rose, intending to seek solace in distance, but first he wanted to know what to expect.

"Is the trial over?" he asked Mary.

"Yes, thank God. Arches was convicted of a long list of crimes. He'll be in jail for years."

"What are your plans now?" he asked, steeling himself to the possibility that he might not see his new niece until she was a teenager, or older.

Mary stood as she fixed her gaze on him. "Emma needs a masculine influence in her life. I was hoping she could get to know her uncle."

He'd expected her to say that she was moving on and blinked back his surprise that she wasn't. Yet he wasn't willing to raise his hopes. "Which means?"

"I'd like to stay in Hope." She glanced at Nikki, then back at him. "If this is where you'll be."

He purposely avoided looking at Nikki. What would be the point of wanting to be with a woman who refused to be honest with him?

"I'm not going anywhere," he said. "Do you have a place to stay?"

"Not yet. I thought Emma and I would go to a hotel until I found a house."

In spite of the blow to his self-esteem, Mary was still his sister. He dug in his pocket, pulled out his car keys and removed one from the ring. "Here's the key to my apartment. You're welcome to live there as long as you like. It isn't anything fancy," he warned, intending to turn his room over to Mary and Emma while he slept on the sofa. He could even bunk down in the doctors' lounge, if necessary.

She accepted the key. "I'm sure it will be fine. Thanks."

He opened the door. "I have to get back to work. Nikki can give you the address and directions."

She nodded.

Galen turned away, then stopped. "For what it's worth, 'm glad you're here," he said simply, then walked away without a backward glance. He might be able to forgive Mary for her choices because she didn't know the man he'd become, but he couldn't overlook Nikki's actions as easily. The one woman who knew him better than anyone else, the one whom he'd trusted to be honest and forthright, had lied by omission.

If Nikki could keep such important information from him, knowing that he was desperate for news about his sister, then what else would she choose not to tell him? He'd never imagined that she could or *would* let him down in such a fashion, but she had, and in the process had brought down the rest of his dreams as well.

Nikki looked at Mary, not sure what to say. If only she'd been able to prepare him for the shock, if only she'd won the gamble she'd taken, but she hadn't. Now she'd lost everything.

Mary's smile seemed forced. "That went better than I'd expected, but I still have a lot to make up for. I really hurt him, didn't I?"

Nikki recalled his bleak expression and the way he'd avoided her gaze. "Not as much as I did."

If she let him walk away, she'd lose the ground they'd gained over the past month. The fear of that happening swelled to choking proportions and left her at the proverbial fork in the road. Did she intend to fight for what she wanted or not? Would she meekly accept his rejection as her due, or would she take a chance and grab for the prize?

"I have to go," she said, rushing to the door. "I have to fix this."

"You love him, don't you?" Mary asked, stopping Nikki in her tracks.

She didn't hesitate. "I do. Completely. In fact, I want to marry him, if he'll have me." Which was why she was so afraid that she'd irrevocably ruined things between them and so desperate to repair the damage she'd caused.

Mary smiled. "I thought so."

Nikki started to rush on, then realized she couldn't leave Mary stranded without knowing her daughter's whereabouts. "Ask Jean to escort you to the day-care center so you can see Emma."

"I will. Thanks. And good luck," Mary called as Nikki increased her pace. Galen had probably returned to the ER, so she'd look for him there first.

And when she found him, she'd do or say whatever was necessary to set their relationship to rights. It would be a time for brutal honesty and heartfelt sincerity.

And what if he won't listen?

Fear of failure threatened her again, but she quickly refused to let it take root. Galen *would* listen to her, she vowed, even if she had to resort to doing something drastic.

She caught up to him just as he was ready to push through the fire doors separating the main ER from the MEC. "Galen! Wait."

He paused, before turning slowly to face her. "What do you want?"

"I want to talk to you."

"Why?" he asked bluntly.

"Because I want to explain."

"Sorry, don't waste your breath."

She dashed in front of him to block his path. "I wasn't sure if Alice really was your sister."

"You weren't sure about the woman on television either," he reminded her. "But that didn't stop you from voicing your suspicions. Or did you think I would some-

ow jeopardize Emma's safety if I knew she was my
niece?''

"No! I was only trying to protect you from being hurt.''

"You had no right to keep something this big a secret
from me. To think I wanted to earn your trust and your
love by showing you mine all this time.'' He shook his
head in obvious disgust. "If keeping secrets and not trust-
ing is what you think love is, I don't want a part of it.''

She froze as his comment sank home. "You love me?''

"Did you think that hearing of your duplicity would
hurt so much if I didn't?''

"I was going to tell you about Mary,'' she reminded
him, more determined than ever to straighten out this mess.
'I tried, remember? But you were taking Melanie to lunch.
And then—''

Galen threw up his hands and turned away. "I don't
know why I'm bothering to discuss this. We're not getting
anywhere.''

"If you go,'' she warned as he started to storm through
the fire doors, "then you aren't as interested in commitment as you claimed.''

He paused. "I just happen to think it's a two-way
street.''

"Which is why if we don't clear the air, we're doomed
to repeat the same mistake we made a year ago. I, for one,
don't want to do that. Not this time.''

He rubbed his face in obvious frustration. "The point
is, I know you're afraid to trust me for fear that I'll make
a promise and still leave you someday, just like your birth
mother did.

"I also know that my track record hasn't been good,''
he continued. "I'd hoped to prove myself through actions
rather than words that I wasn't like my father and could
handle the responsibility of a family.''

She interrupted. "Handle responsibility? Prove your willingness to settle down through your actions? Then why didn't you move in me with when I asked you?"

"Because I was trying to measure up to your brothers!" he roared. "They were the ones who protected you and always looked out for your best interests, but I've since learned it's impossible. You'll never trust me the same way you trust them."

Measure up to her brothers? Suddenly the cogs began to click into place. It had been his own determination to be honorable, to prove his worthiness to her brothers, that had stopped him from taking what she'd so freely offered to him a year ago. And now, twelve months later, he was doing the same thing.

"Do you realize we've come full circle?" she asked quietly.

He raised an eyebrow. "What are you talking about?"

"Your integrity caused you to walk away from me a year ago and has kept you from choosing to move in now. Unfortunately, by using the question as a test of your willingness to go the distance, I expected you to sacrifice the very thing you were trying to prove and protect." She shook her head. "We were setting ourselves up to be at odds with each other, and we simply didn't know it.

"That's what we're really arguing about," she added. "Maybe I did keep a secret from you, but I was trying to save you some grief. In the end I only made it worse and I'm sorry, but I had pure motives and you can't fault me for that."

He let out a deep sigh and his shoulders slumped. " suppose not."

"Furthermore," she added quietly, "I never needed you to measure up to my brothers. My love gives you an extra advantage and tips the scales in your favor."

A smile slowly stretched across Galen's face. "It oes?"

Nikki stepped closer. "Yes, it does. And since you seem o be dragging your feet about asking me an important uestion, I'll ask you. Will you marry me and my five nosy rothers?"

He opened his arms and enfolded her in a big hug. "Yeah. I love you, Nik. For ever and ever."

She smiled and waited for his kiss. She'd never heard ner words or received a better promise.

Modern Romance™
...international affairs – seduction and passion guaranteed

Medical Romance™
...pulse-raising romance – heart-racing medical drama

Tender Romance™
...sparkling, emotional, feel-good romance

Sensual Romance™
...teasing, tempting, provocatively playful

Historical Romance™
...rich, vivid and passionate

Blaze Romance™
...scorching hot sexy reads

27 new titles every month.

Live the emotion

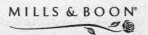

MILLS & BOON®

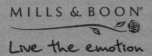

MILLS & BOON®

Live the emotion

Medical Romance™

LIKE DOCTOR, LIKE SON *by Josie Metcalfe*

He had a son – nearly grown, and so like him in looks and intention as to want to be a doctor too. GP Quinn Jamison knew that more than pregnancy must have kept Faith away from him for so many years – he couldn't believe she had fallen out of love with him any more than he had stopped loving her. Did he now have a chance to discover the truth?

THE A&E CONSULTANT'S SECRET *by Lilian Darcy*
Glenfallon

At eighteen years old Nell Cassidy was forced to give up her first love – Bren Forsythe. Now she's a successful A&E consultant, back in Glenfallon, and Bren is the new surgeon! Soon he rediscovers the fiery, passionate woman he remembers, and Nell wants nothing more than to open her heart to him. But first she has to tell him why she let him go…

THE DOCTOR'S SPECIAL CHARM *by Laura MacDonald*
Eleanor James Memorial

Dr Sandie Rawlings is faced with a challenge on the paediatrics ward – the gorgeous new registrar, Dr Omar Nahum. Omar has a reputation as a heartbreaker, and Sandie is certain she won't fall for his seductive charm. But when Omar makes it clear that she's something special to him, all her certainties disappear!

On sale 2nd July 2004

Available at most branches of WHSmith, Tesco, Martins, Borders, Eason, Sainsbury's and all good paperback bookshops.

0604/03a

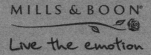

MILLS & BOON®

Live the emotion

Medical Romance™

DR FELLINI'S PREGNANT BRIDE by *Margaret Barker*
Roman Hospital

Dr Sarah Montgomery discovered she was pregnant by her ex-boyfriend just before joining the A&E department of a hospital in Rome. Life would be complicated enough without her falling for her new boss, consultant Carlos Fellini! But the desire Carlos felt for Sarah did not lessen with her news – it made him more protective…

THE ENGLISH DOCTOR'S DILEMMA by *Lucy Clark*

When English doctor Elizabeth Blakeny-Smith takes a job in the Outback, she's hoping to take control of her life. But a kiss from a sexy stranger sends her pulse racing, and suddenly control is the last thing on her mind! Then she discovers that the stranger is her new colleague, Dr Mitch O'Neill…

THE SPANISH CONSULTANT'S BABY by *Kate Hardy*
Mediterranean Doctors

Nurse Jennifer Jacobs can't help being attracted to new doctor Ramón Martínez, but after an unhappy marriage she's vowed never to wed again. Ramón makes no secret of his passion for Jennifer, and as they're forced to work closely together she gives in to temptation. But desire soon has life-changing consequences: Jennifer is pregnant!

On sale 2nd July 2004

FREE

4 BOOKS
AND A SURPRISE GIFT!

We would like to take this opportunity to thank you for reading this Mills & Boon® book b
offering you the chance to take FOUR more specially selected titles from the Medical Romance™
series absolutely FREE! We're also making this offer to introduce you to the benefits o
the Reader Service™—

★ FREE home delivery   ★ FREE gifts and competitions
★ FREE monthly Newsletter   ★ Exclusive Reader Service discount
★ Books available before they're in the shops

Accepting these FREE books and gift places you under no obligation to buy; you may cance
at any time, even after receiving your free shipment. Simply complete your details below an
return the entire page to the address below. **You don't even need a stamp!**

YES! Please send me 4 free Medical Romance books and a surprise gift. I understand tha
unless you hear from me, I will receive 6 superb new titles every month for just £2.6
each, postage and packing free. I am under no obligation to purchase any books and may cance
my subscription at any time. The free books and gift will be mine to keep in any case.

M4ZEF

Ms/Mrs/Miss/Mr ....Initials ....
BLOCK CAPITALS PLEA'

Surname ....

Address ....

....

....Postcode ....

Send this whole page to:
UK: FREEPOST CN81, Croydon, CR9 3WZ
EIRE: PO Box 4546, Kilcock, County Kildare (stamp required)

Offer valid in UK and Eire only and not available to current Reader Service subscribers to this series. We reserve the right
refuse an application and applicants must be aged 18 years or over. Only one application per household. Terms and pric
subject to change without notice. Offer expires 30th September 2004. As a result of this application, you may receive offers fro
Harlequin Mills & Boon and other carefully selected companies. If you would prefer not to share in this opportunity please write
The Data Manager at PO Box 676, Richmond, TW9 1WU.

Mills & Boon® is a registered trademark owned by Harlequin Mills & Boon Limited.
Medical Romance™ is being used as a trademark.
The Reader Service™ is being used as a trademark.